She looked at the [illegible] single tall pillar of gr[illegible] an acre of asphalt.

A lonely pillar. “I wish I was as good as you are at imagining that everything will work out okay.”

He turned toward her, laying his arm along the back of the bench. She was aware that his hand rested on the bench just behind her shoulder blades, right behind her spine, the very spine she needed to stiffen.

“Is everything not okay with you?” he asked.

She didn’t want to have a spine of steel. She wanted to melt into his arms. “Isn’t everything not okay with everyone? We all have our little troubles, right? Everyone’s fighting their own battle.”

She was babbling, fighting the desire to lean into him, into Alex Gregory, MD, according to the embroidery on his coat. *Can I call you Alex? Tell you all my worries?*

“Grace, you can talk to me.”

Okay, that was a little scary. He was like the perfect guy.

But he was studying her again. She didn’t know when anyone else had ever looked at her so closely. She was only an assistant, for goodness’ sake. Keeper of the lipstick and the schedule. What was there for him to see?

TEXAS RESCUE:
Rescuing hearts...one Texan at a time!

Dear Reader,

I hope you enjoy reading this romance as much as I enjoyed writing the happily-ever-after ending. This hero particularly deserved to end up with the perfect woman for him, a heroine who is an optimist at her core. Of course, every hero deserves his heroine at the end, but I have a particular soft spot for this hero. He's a doctor in an emergency room, and I felt I understood him because of my own experiences.

You see, once upon a time, I was in emergency services as a police officer. I became accustomed to the fact that every single call I answered, every single person I spoke to, was in trouble, whether they were victims, suspects—or just lost and needing directions! When I was off duty, that feeling persisted. If I saw a car at the side of the road, I assumed the driver needed my help. Always. This emergency-room hero feels the same way. Every day, all the people he interacts with need him to fix their problems, so when he meets the heroine, he assumes she needs his help, as well. Part of the happily-ever-after includes the hero's realization that the heroine doesn't need him—but she does want him. Her personal strength is as appealing to him as her pretty face.

I'd love to hear your thoughts on this story. You can find me as Caro Carson on Facebook and Twitter, or you can drop me a private email through my website at carocarson.com.

Cheers,

Caro Carson

Her Texas Rescue Doctor

Caro Carson

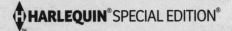

HARLEQUIN®SPECIAL EDITION®

Recycling programs
for this product may
not exist in your area.

ISBN-13: 978-0-373-65981-4

Her Texas Rescue Doctor

Copyright © 2016 by Caro Carson

Printed in U.S.A.

TM www.Harlequin.com

Despite a no-nonsense background as a West Point graduate and US Army officer, **Caro Carson** has always treasured the happily-ever-after of a good romance novel. Now Caro is delighted to be living her own happily-ever-after with her husband and two children in the great state of Florida, a location that has saved the coaster-loving theme-park fanatic a fortune on plane tickets.

This book is dedicated to my mother in-law, Ilse, a woman who lives every day expecting happiness and good things. She deserves them.

Chapter One

"Sophia, you have to put down your phone."

"No."

Grace Jackson gritted her teeth and held out her hand. "Yes, Sophia. Let me have it."

Sophia tossed her blond hair, the perfect platinum blond that belonged to innocent young children, and jerked her phone out of Grace's reach.

Grace struggled for patience. They were in a parked van. How long did Sophia think she could play keep-away with the phone? Sophia had never been easy to deal with, but this phase was particularly trying. At least, Grace hoped it was a phase.

Please, let this be a phase. I can't survive this much longer.

"Look, Sophie. The firemen are waiting for us over there. They want to show you around."

"Don't care."

Grace felt a little desperate. She thought about grabbing

the phone, but taking a hard line with Sophia always back-fired. For the past year, she'd been able to manage Sophia by persuading her with rewards. *If you do this, you'll get that thing you want...* It was as simple as rewarding a tod-dler with a lollipop.

If only Sophia were a toddler.

Instead, Grace was trying to reason with a twenty-nine-year-old woman, a professional actress. After a decade of hard work, Sophia was now a genuine movie star. Grace had been her personal assistant through the hard times, the desperate times, the my-dream-will-never-come-true times. For the past two years, Grace had been with her for the even more stressful world of success, both critical and commercial. The world was Sophia's oyster. And now...

Grace glared at the top of Sophia's head, which was all she could see as Sophia sat on a bench opposite to her with her nose in her phone's screen.

And now, there was no way in the world that Grace was going to placidly stand by and watch Sophia destroy her own dreams.

Grace snatched the phone out of Sophia's hand.

"Hey!"

"I'll hold it for you. What's a personal assistant for?" She slid the phone into her tote bag. "The cameras are waiting. Photographers are everywhere out there. Smile."

Sophie bared her teeth at Grace despite her annoyance; years of habit were hard to break.

"No lipstick on your teeth. No spinach." Grace reached with two hands to fluff Sophia's shining waves and used her fingertips to arrange a few naturally wavy tendrils along Sophia's flawless cheekbones. "Perfect. I see a ton of teenage girls out there. Pose for some selfies with them, okay? A few minutes of smiles, and Sophia Jackson will start trending on Instagram and Twitter again."

But Sophia didn't want her lollipop anymore. She didn't

want to be a respected actress with a loyal fan base, not since she'd fallen in with the bad boys of Hollywood. "Let's skip the squealing mass of girlies. What do I have to do before we can get the hell out of here?"

"Oh, Sophie." Grace's heart felt like a stone in her chest. It was a hard thing, very hard, to watch Sophia throw away everything for which she'd worked.

"Don't start with me. What am I required to do? Tell me the bare minimum. I'm so freaking tired."

Grace supposed clubbing all night could do that to a girl. Sophie coughed that annoying cough that had started shortly after dating Deezee Kalm, a DJ in Los Angeles. Grace always felt like she was choking on the secondhand smoke at his parties, when she was forced to go. Thankfully, Sophie hadn't been photographed with a cigarette in her hand yet. Accusations would fly that she was a bad role model. That would tarnish her good-girl image, the very image Grace was trying to save with this trip to Texas.

"This is a really good cause. Texas Rescue and Relief has done so much here in Austin after those terrible flash floods last summer. You're going to thank the firemen and the— the helicopter people, whatever they're called—and some doctors, and then you're going to cut the ribbon to reopen this health clinic."

"Good God, Grace. Could you have booked anything more stupid?"

The stone in Grace's chest wasn't hard enough to deflect that stab of a knife. *Don't confront her. Don't challenge her. Offer her a lollipop.*

"Your hero, Julia, did almost the exact same thing after California's forest fires. She trended on Twitter. Her visit was covered on all the celebrity gossip TV shows. Now her next movie is already getting award buzz, and it won't be released for months. Coincidence? No way."

Grace reached up to touch Sophia's hair again, a comforting gesture she'd been doing her whole life. After all, she wasn't just Sophia's personal assistant. She was her sister.

Grace would be the worst sister in the world if she stood by and watched her sister self-destruct.

"I've already got a Golden Globe," Sophia said.

"Julia's got two. And an Oscar." Grace nodded out the window toward the cluster of Texas Rescue personnel who were setting up the ribbon-cutting ceremony. "Go be Sophia Jackson, talented and gracious. You could jump in there and help set up right now. Everyone would talk about how down-to-earth you are, how you don't stand on ceremony."

But her superstar sister's cell phone chimed in the tote bag.

Sophia snapped her gum. "Or you could give me my phone so I'm not stuck in the middle of nowhere with nobody to talk to."

"Austin isn't nowhere."

And when did I become nobody?

Instead of defending herself, Grace defended their location. "Austin is a hot ticket in March, you know. It wasn't easy to get a hotel room because South by Southwest just started. The director of Texas Rescue had to call in some favors in town."

Sophia glared at her.

"You know South by Southwest. The fringe festival. Bands, indie movies, art—kind of edgy stuff. Why don't I get the hotel to extend our stay for the week? This is a really hip event. We could have fun."

"I know what the hell South by Southwest is. I just don't care."

Grace had always been the one who listened while Sophia brainstormed career goals. Grace tried to start a little session now. "Being seen here might add another dimension to your image. People might start thinking of you for projects that have more of an indie vibe, like a *Juno* or a *Fargo*."

"I am not sticking around here for a week of low-budget fringe films, and I'm not going out there to cut a stupid ribbon until I absolutely have to."

Grace knew better than to push the point. "Okay, we'll chill out here in their van until they're ready for you. Then you can go and shake hands like you're Kate Middleton. They'll love you, the studios will love you, and your agent will get you the best roles in the industry."

"Are little bluebirds going to start circling my head while I act like a princess? This is seriously stupid." Sophia gestured toward Grace's tote bag. "Check and see if that's Deezee on the phone. He wants me. Tonight."

"He wants you? You mean…like…a booty call? He actually calls you to tell you when he wants…" Grace couldn't finish the sentence.

"You are so last decade. *Booty* just means butt. By the way, Deezee says the bubble butt is last decade, so I'm not going to get the surgery now."

Grace felt ill. She didn't know Sophia had even considered having a plastic surgeon implant anything in her naturally perfect figure.

"He can tell if a girl's had implants during sex. He's so impressed that I haven't had any work done yet."

Grace wanted to stick her fingers in her ears and say *not listening*, just as she had when they were children and Sophia had explained the birds and bees to her. "I don't want to hear about his sexual turn-ons."

"Then stop being obsessed with my phone calls. Get your own sex life. When's the last time you got any?" She shoved Grace's tote bag with the toe of her spike-heeled sandal. "Back when people still used the term *booty call*, I guess."

Grace had to look away. Her sister, of all people, ought

to know that she had no social life. Managing all the little daily details for Sophia was a never-ending job. Sophia's career dictated where they lived, who they saw, what they did—even what Grace wore. Her wardrobe consisted of dozens of outfits like the gray sweater and slacks she wore now. Years ago, she and her sister had figured out that wearing all black made Grace appear like a noticeable blot of darkness when she was caught in the background of a candid photo of Sophia, so Grace wore earth tones with a bit of heather, or sometimes gray with specks of beige and black. That was the best way to disappear into the background.

Not that Grace was complaining. She loved her sister. She only wished her sister would go back to being her normal self. When they were a sisterly duo, she hadn't minded living Sophia's life. This new phase was making her question everything.

She pretended the view outside the van was interesting, but the restored health clinic was only a normal-sized building in a normal suburb of a normal city. The ribbon-cutting ceremony was about to begin, so the men and women of Texas Rescue were taking their places.

She'd bet those people were married and had children and rewarding jobs. Grace and Sophia had once had that kind of normalcy, back when their parents were still alive. How could Sophia go from seeing their parents' loving marriage to jumping at the beck and call of a no-talent egomaniac like Deezee?

Of the two of them, Sophia had always been the bigger sucker for true love and weddings and happily-ever-after. She'd put all that on hold for her acting career, until this winter with Deezee. Maybe this phase meant Sophia was lonely. Maybe Grace could help her find a better man. A normal man.

Grace gestured out the window. "Check out these Texas Rescue guys. This looks like a casting call for an action movie—but they're real. I bet not one of those guys has chin implants or hair extensions. Real firemen and real doctors and paramedics and, um, police-looking guys. Rangers? What do you think that uniform is?"

"Like I care." Sophia sat up straighter, ready to talk business. "Listen, Deezee is opening a new club tonight. He needs me there to help him get more press."

Grace looked away from the handsome men of the real world. If Sophia wanted to talk business, they'd talk business. "Deezee could have his people contact me with a little more notice next time, and maybe we'll be able to schedule an appearance, if his career needs help."

Sophia's expressive blue eyes narrowed angrily, but a fresh round of her club cough kept her from saying whatever retort she'd been about to deliver.

Poor Sophia really did look tired. It was up to her personal assistant to help her look good for this photo op, so Grace dug in her tote bag and came up with her sister's very expensive, very red lipstick, the one Grace ordered for her and always kept on hand. "Here. And spit out your gum. It looks tacky when you speak."

Sophia's cough subsided. "Being with Deezee can do more for my career than this charity gig. Everyone will be in LA at the new club. No one is here. If you want me to stay visible in the industry, I need to be where everyone is. *Duh*." Sophia plucked the lipstick out of Grace's fingers.

Grace dropped her hand to her lap. Couldn't Sophia see that Deezee's club would attract the celebrities who were famous only for their ability to shock the public? Actresses would get out of their limos in a way that let the paparazzi document whether or not they wore underwear. Stars who were claiming sobriety would arrive drunk.

A man in a shirt and tie opened the door to the van. "Miss Jackson? Are you ready for your tour?"

Sophia ignored him as she gave Grace orders. "Book

me a flight. Get me back to LA now. I'm going to cut this crap short."

Grace closed her eyes, but it didn't matter. She heard the man at the door suck in his breath.

Surprise. She's a little more crude in real life than she was in her award acceptance speech, isn't she?

Grace opened her eyes and looked at the man's face. Yep. They'd just alienated another fan.

For the past two years, Sophia had been so gracious in her interviews, so fun on her television appearances. She'd set a goal to be as well thought of as Audrey Hepburn someday, and she'd pursued her dream with unwavering perseverance until now. Audrey Hepburn wouldn't have told a Texas Rescue volunteer that she wanted to cut this crap short.

DJ Deezee Kalm would have, except he wouldn't have used the word *crap*.

Sophia replaced the cap on her lipstick and tossed it so that it landed on the bench seat next to Grace.

"Your gum," Grace reminded her gently, under her breath.

"Get me a limo to the airport. This van blows." Sophia tilted her head back, pursed her lips, and with a poof of air, spit her gum to land on the seat, as well.

She got out of the van. Grace watched out the window as Sophia shook back her hair in the Texas sunlight, looking like a million dollars in a classic coat dress that cost eight thousand. Grace had secured it at no cost. The publicity Sophia could bring a designer was worth more than the price of the dress. For now.

The adults applauded, the teenaged girls who crowded against the plastic barricades screamed and cheered, but Sophia didn't walk over to her waiting fans. Grace wished she hadn't suggested it. Maybe her sister would have done the obviously right thing if she hadn't felt like Grace was ordering her to do it.

Grace picked up the lipstick and returned it to the tote, then dug out a tissue and cleaned up the gum. *What's a personal assistant for, right?*

Not this. She'd been her sister's support, not her sister's servant. But her sister was no longer acting like her sister. Sophia was turning herself into something she was not, all in an attempt to make a man love her.

Deezee didn't love her—but Grace did. She'd dragged her from LA to Texas for her own good. Surely Sophia would come to her senses. Grace just had to find a way to keep her in Texas a little longer.

She sighed and looked out the window again, at the group of handsome men who were all shaking her sister's hand. What if, instead of a Hollywood bad boy, Sophia fell for one of these men? Maybe one of the doctors, someone who was caring by nature, someone whose profession meant he was successful and respected, independent of her sister's success. Wouldn't it be lovely if Sophia fell in love with a guy like that? It would cure all their ills.

A handsome man from Texas Rescue could be just what the doctor ordered.

"Hi, I'm Dr. Gregory."

Alex Gregory, MD, held his hand out to shake with the young boy who'd come to his emergency room with a sports injury.

The child's father grabbed Alex's hand instead and squeezed. Hard. "What took you so long, Doc?"

"I'm sorry for your wait. Things are unpredictable around here." Alex extricated his hand from the bone-crushing grip. To restore some circulation, he made a fist and used one knuckle to push his glasses farther up the bridge of his nose. Then he spread his fingers out wide, and made a second attempt to engage his young patient.

"So, I'm Dr. Gregory, you're Justin, and I hear that you came in because you got hurt. Can you tell me where?"

"It's his leg, Doc. He's got a big game tomorrow. We need you to patch him up to get him through. Maybe a cortisone shot and a knee brace."

Alex kept his expression neutral for the sake of the little boy on the gurney. According to the chart, the child was eight years old. This parent was acting like his kid was an NFL superstar. "Justin, can you tell me where it hurts?"

The child looked up at him silently and pointed at his left leg.

"Okay, I'll check out your leg. Anywhere else I should look?"

"My chin hurts, too. I hit it right here, and—"

"Just tell him the important stuff, son. Shake off the little things, like a man."

Take it down a notch, Bubba. That was what Alex wanted to say. As Dr. Gregory, of course, he didn't. Part of every accident evaluation included screening for head trauma, particularly since this child had just reported that he'd sustained a hit to the chin. The screening could be as simple as listening to the child relate his injuries logically and with clear speech.

In other words, the father needed to shut up.

Alex crossed to the sink and washed his hands in preparation for an exam. His little patient was so miserable and tense, manipulating that injured leg was going to be an ordeal, unless he could get the child to relax at least a little bit. Confronting his father would only make the child more tense.

Alex began drying his hands on rough brown paper towels. "So, Justin, how'd you hurt your leg?"

"S-s-soccer."

"He was playing an aggressive forward position and he—"

Enough. Alex turned abruptly to face the father. In silence, he held the man's gaze. It helped that Alex was as tall as the father. He certainly lacked the beer belly, but he looked ol' Bubba in the eye. With his back to the boy, Alex let his expression show his disapproval as he dried his hands.

"—and he cut the ball back to this rookie, who…ah…" The father's monologue came to a confused halt under Alex's glare.

Alex crushed the paper towels into a ball and pitched them into the trash can. Deliberately, taking his time, Alex pointed at the chair in the corner. The father sank slowly into the empty chair.

Alex turned back to Justin. He started with the child's arm, knowing it was uninjured and wouldn't cause him any pain while he lifted it and bent the elbow, testing the range of motion, a way to let the child get familiar with the exam. "Do you play any other sports?"

The child darted a fearful glance at his father, making sure it was okay to talk. "Dad coaches me in basketball, too. Right, Dad?"

Dad hesitated and glanced at Alex before answering. "And baseball. We're doing baseball this year."

Justin looked from his father back to Alex. "And b-baseball."

"Wow, that's a lot of sports." Alex hadn't missed the child's fearful glance. He took his stethoscope off his neck. It gave him the perfect excuse to lift the boy's shirt to listen to his heart. He'd be looking for bruises, too. Usually, an overbearing soccer dad was just that, but sometimes that overbearing personality became violent, and children could be the victims.

"What sports do you do?" the boy asked.

Alex smiled a bit. Kids only knew their own worlds. If their world was an endless cycle of practices and games, they assumed everyone was involved in sports. Thankfully, little Justin had no bruises. His life with his dad centered on sports whether he liked it or not, but it appeared his life was free of physical violence. Not like Alex's had once been.

"I'm not on any teams like you are. I ride my bike a lot, though."

He could've felt the father's derision even if he hadn't heard the snort of disgust. Alex was used to it from a certain type of man. Alex had been raised in Europe, in the dangerous, crumbling Soviet Bloc. The best moments of his grim childhood had been seeing the professional cyclists in their brightly colored kits go whizzing through his town, training for the Tour de France. When Alex had escaped to America as a teen, he'd been shocked that his new schoolmates didn't know any pro cyclists by name.

"I can ride a two-wheeler," Justin said.

"Yeah? That's great." Alex started palpating the child's good leg, picking up the diminutive foot in his hand and rotating it to test the ankle. "Do you have a favorite movie?"

The kid lit up like a lightbulb. "I like *Star Wars*. Do you know that one? And I like *Guardians of the Galaxy*. And I like *Space Maze*."

"I'm going to bend your knee now." Alex wanted to keep Justin focused on something else. "Who's your favorite character out of the whole Maze world?"

"I like Eva. You know, Princess Picasso."

Dad snorted again. "A princess? Goya the Destroya, that was the best guy in the movie."

"But Dad, Goya was a bad guy. Eva was the good guy." Justin looked ready to cry, and Alex didn't think it was because his leg hurt him.

"So what? Goya kicked azzz…uh, butt."

Justin showed a little spark of defiance. "Eva had a cool laser gun. She kept it hidden in her boot."

Good for you, kid. You're going to need that stubbornness with a father like yours.

Alex had liked the Eva Picasso character, too. "She was really brave. She saved her people from the maze. I'm going to need you to be really brave for a minute. I'm going to move your knee as far as it will go." It was a matter of millimeters before Justin responded in pain and Alex stopped. He patted the kid on his good leg. "Do you remember what the princess kept in her other boot?"

Justin's grimace relaxed a bit. "Yeah, that really cool knife that could cut right through anything. Even metal."

"You're talking 'bout the chick who wore the boots?" His father sat back, sounding relieved. "She was hot. Sophia Jackson, that's the one. Okay, yeah, the boots chick was hot."

"And brave," Justin said.

"And brave," Alex agreed as he stood up. "I don't think the bone in your leg is broken, but I need to get an X-ray to be sure. It won't hurt. An X-ray is a special kind of camera."

"I know," Justin said. "It can take a picture right through your clothes. Princess Picasso could get one with her boots on."

Dear old Dad couldn't help himself. "I bet the doc would love to get a picture of Sophia Jackson right through her clothes. Who wouldn't? Am I right?"

Alex didn't reply. What he'd like to see was Princess Picasso giving this Neanderthal one of her go-to-hell looks.

A brave princess in his ER?

That would make his day.

Chapter Two

Grace was a coward. She darted a glance around the van, petrified of getting caught.

Don't be such a scaredy-cat. All eyes are on Sophia, anyway.

Grace pulled her sister's phone out of her bag. What she was about to do was for Sophia's own good. When the lock screen lit up, she tapped in the four-digit access code.

It was rejected.

The code was supposed to be the year Grace had been born. Although it surprised the few people who learned of it, Grace was actually the baby sister, only twenty-five to Sophia's twenty-nine. Her big sister loved her. Her big sister used baby Grace's birth year as her code. Only it didn't work now.

How old was Deezee? Grace typed in his birth year. It worked.

The stab to her heart was starting to feel too familiar.

With jaw clenched, Grace began deleting photos, horrible shots of her sister's bare breasts covered by Deezee's hands, shots that would never, ever end up on Instagram, not when she could prevent it.

Delete, delete, delete.

The van doors opened with a sudden rush of air. Grace dropped her sister's phone like a hot potato.

A woman about her own age poked her head in. "Hi. You're with Sophia Jackson, right?"

"Yes." She blinked in what she hoped was an innocent way.

"There's been an accident."

For one horrible moment, the world stopped.

An accident. Careers and reputations and idiot boyfriends evaporated before the image of a hurt Sophia.

"Oh, my God." The words were a whisper, but inside her head she was screaming. *My sister, my sister!* Their parents had been killed in a car accident. A stranger, a woman like this one, had come just this kindly to tell them there had been an accident. Grace had been fifteen. Sophia had been nineteen.

"It's nothing life threatening, I promise. We have so many Texas Rescue doctors and paramedics and firefighters here, she's being well taken care of, but they do think she should go to the hospital to have things checked out."

The only reason Grace had survived the loss of her parents was because Sophia had been by her side, taking on the role of parent, loving her with all she had. But now Sophia had been in an accident, hurt badly enough that she needed to go to the emergency room. *My sister, my sister!*

"Would you like to ride in the ambulance with her?"

Grace clutched her tote bag as she scrambled out of the van. The fans behind the barricade were silent, wide-eyed. The yellow ribbon had been cut. Its ends flapped in the light breeze as the ceremonial scissors leaned against the building, standing on their points, forgotten. All the men and women in suits and uniforms were now by the open doors to an ambulance. The kind woman escorted Grace right through the little cluster. A paramedic offered her a hand up, and there Sophia lay, looking miserable on a gurney. Miserable, but very much alive.

Grace threw herself onto her big sister for a hug. "Are you okay?"

Sophia put her hand on her shoulder—and gave her a shove. "Don't bump my leg. I'm going to sue somebody if this makes me miss Deezee's party. Give me my phone. I need to call him. He's going to freak when he sees this on Instagram."

Deezee was going to be worried? *What about me?*

While Sophia lapsed into another coughing fit, Grace sat on the metal bench that ran the length of the ambulance's interior. She slid her tote bag closer, slowly, buying herself time to get her emotions under control. For all of her life, she'd been the one whom Sophia had worried about. After their parents had died, they'd been afraid to be apart, afraid of the future—afraid they'd lose each other in a split second, the way they'd lost their parents. Sophia had let Grace crawl into her bed when she was afraid of the dark.

"You know, when they said you were in an accident just now, all I could think of was Mom and Dad…" The words hurt her throat.

Sophia went still and looked at her, really looked at her for the first time in ages. "Aw, Gracie." And then, also for the first time in ages, it was her sister who reached out to fix her hair, smoothing Grace's plain brown hair over her shoulder. It had once been blond like Sophia's but had darkened in adulthood.

A paramedic jumped into the bay with them, a man

who could get work as a body double for Thor. Grace said hello; Sophia ignored him. Doors slammed shut, and the ambulance began moving.

The cell phone in her tote bag rang. Her sister practically jackknifed into a sitting position on the gurney, which immediately made her yelp in pain and freeze in place. Still, she could give an order through clenched teeth. "Answer it. Hurry."

"It's mine." Grace dug in her bag and silenced the ring.

"Hand me mine. Maybe Deezee called."

Deezee never called. Sophia was to do the work. Sophia was to come and see him, at his convenience, without any notice. If Deezee saw a photo on Twitter or Instagram of Sophia being loaded into the back of an ambulance, he'd expect Sophia to call him and tell him the latest. Didn't she realize that?

Sophia held out her hand and made a little grabby motion. "He'll get pissed if I don't tell him what's going on. He'll want to know what hospital I'm at."

Or maybe Sophia did realize how little effort Deezee made, and she just didn't know that wasn't normal. Maybe she'd forgotten how Dad had treated Mom, once upon a time.

At any rate, Grace didn't have Sophia's phone. She'd tossed it aside in her haste to make sure Sophia wasn't dying. She couldn't say that, though. The phone should have been in her tote bag, not in her hand.

"It must have fallen out of my bag in the van."

"You *lost* my phone?"

The paramedic chose that moment to interrupt by wrapping the black Velcro of a blood pressure cuff around Sophia's upper arm. "Let's get your blood pressure."

Grace tried to reassure her sister. "I'm pretty sure I remember seeing it lying on the seat with your lipstick, actually."

Sophia laid back with a huff, her life so inconvenienced by a handsome paramedic who was taking care of her. She glared at Grace, looking pretty fearsome for someone who was hurt badly enough to be in the back of an ambulance at the moment.

"It'll be okay. We know it's in the van, and I'm sure the Texas Rescue people will find it and bring it back to the hospital."

"They'll look at my personal stuff. You're the one who is always so worried about what will get out on social media. You think those Texas Rescue people aren't going to pass around Sophia Jackson's personal phone for kicks and giggles?"

The paramedic didn't like that, Grace could tell from the way he clenched his jaw. Neither did she. She wouldn't lose her temper, though. Confronting Sophia never worked.

"They can't see what's in your phone." She spoke as sweetly as possible, but she knew it sounded fake. It was her sister who was the actress, after all. "You have your phone locked. Our special secret sister code is still protecting it, right?"

Sophia opened her mouth, then shut it again, and looked at her through narrowed eyes. "Of course."

The wall between them seemed just a little higher. Just a little harder to breach. It was a wall in the shape of a man. A stupid, worthless type of man, who was systematically pushing Grace out of her sister's life.

Grace couldn't imagine being so blind in love. If she were to fall in love, one thing was for certain: she would never, ever love a man who didn't also love her sister.

Alex Gregory hated Sophia Jackson.

It was a shame, because she'd been a good actress in some excellent films. He'd be blind not to think she was attractive, but it had taken less than two sentences to determine that the person behind the famous face was rude and shallow.

"Good afternoon. I'm Dr. Gregory."

"What took you so long?"

Rude.

But no more rude than young Justin's father. Alex had pushed his glasses farther up his nose. "That seems to be a popular question this afternoon. We're a little busier than usual during South by Southwest. What's brought you in today?"

"Where the hell is my phone?"

And shallow.

Nothing during the exam was changing his first impression of her. While he examined her ankle, she complained about the facility. She'd been placed in the overflow area, an older part of the emergency department where the beds were separated by curtains rather than walls. This was, according to the not-so-noble woman who'd provided the noble face of Princess Eva Picasso, utterly unacceptable.

"It's also unavoidable," Alex said. "By definition, *overflow area* implies that all the other rooms are full."

"When my personal assistant gets back with my phone, she'll have me moved."

Alex raised an eyebrow on that one. Not many patients brought along a personal assistant, at least not this far from Hollywood. Still, a movie star's personal assistant had exactly zero influence on how the emergency department of West Central Texas Hospital ran. Alex took the stethoscope from around his neck and inserted the ear pieces.

"Oh, no, you don't. You don't get to slip your hand inside this dress. It's my ankle that hurts. Do you think I don't know that you're dying to tell everyone that you felt me up?" Her indignation dissolved into yet another coughing fit.

Sarcastic comments flashed through his mind. *You're right. The stethoscope works just fine if I stand three feet away and aim it at you. We doctors have been lying about that for centuries, but you're the one who figured it out.*

But he was here to provide medical care for a twenty-nine-year-old female patient, not to teach a lesson in sarcasm to a movie star. "I'll be able to hear your lungs through the material. Would you like for me to call in a nurse anyway?"

She crossed her arms over her chest, but leaned forward a few inches, granting him limited access. "You can listen to my back. Then go see if my assistant has found my phone yet. Your Texas Rescue people are probably hiding it from her."

Just provide medical care. Alex put the chest piece on her back, which felt like the back of any other human, whether male or female, attractive or ugly, famous or obscure. *Provide care, then get her out of here.*

He heard the crackles he'd expected to hear. He flipped the stethoscope to hang around the back of his neck again, then slid the curtains back on their metal rings. "We need to get some X-rays, but you won't have to move to a wheelchair. An orderly will roll your gurney down to radiology. There's a bit of a wait right now, but the nurse will be in to check on you periodically."

"You're planning on wheeling me around the hospital in this bed? No, no, no. You need to bring an X-ray machine up here, right after you put me in my own room."

"That's not the way it works here."

"My privacy needs to be guaranteed. Be sure you send my assistant back as soon as you see her. She'll handle everything."

Alex left without another word, snapping the curtains shut behind him. If Sophia Jackson had that much faith in her assistant's ability to make a hospital bow to her whims, then that assistant must be even more of a harridan than Sophia herself. Dr. Gregory planned to steer clear of her. As the only doctor on duty, he didn't have time to spend deflating some puffed-up bit of Hollywood hot air.

His most senior nurse, Loretta, was coming on duty. He'd let Loretta handle Sophia Jackson's personal assistant.

Alex wanted nothing to do with her.

Chapter Three

"Dr. Gregory, we have a problem."

Alex kept writing his notes on the patient in room three, but he nodded to his nurse to continue. Loretta had worked in the ER for so long that nothing shook her up. If Loretta was concerned, then Alex was concerned.

"Go ahead," he said, as he signed his name for the twentieth time today and tossed the paper into the in-box on the nurse's station.

"They just roomed another patient in the overflow area."

"That makes two. The overflow area holds eight."

"I know, but the beds are only separated by curtains in overflow." Loretta lowered her voice as if she were about to tell a secret. "Sophia Jackson is in one of those beds. We'd better do some rearranging. Her assistant is asking about HIPAA."

HIPAA, or *hippah*, as everyone called it, governed medical privacy. The harridan of a personal assistant had arrived, and now she wanted to threaten his ER with privacy regulations, did she?

"You know that the curtained area is considered HIPAA compliant."

"Yes, but Sophia Jackson is *famous*."

Surely his best nurse didn't expect him to move a patient just to pander to someone famous. For the second time this shift, he felt as he had when he'd first come to America. The culture shock had been extreme. To survive the jungle that was the American high school, he'd quickly dumped his cycling stars and learned who the heroes of American football were. He'd killed all trace of his Russian accent. He'd worn blue jeans and Dallas Cowboy T-shirts, but all of that had been camouflage. Surface-level changes.

Deep down, he'd never quite caught that American mindset. To this day, he didn't understand the fascination with the famous. Of all the traits a person might have, fame was one of the most useless. In his old life, rank in the political hierarchy mattered. Wealth mattered, for money bought power, and both could assure safety. Smarts mattered—a smart man could be valuable to those who held rank. But fame? Fame didn't put bread in your belly when you were hiding from corrupt government officials. Fame didn't pay for passage on a rickety ship to a country that didn't want you.

"You know people will overhear you," Loretta said.

"Then I'll try not to call out her full name too loudly as I ask for her autograph."

"Be serious, Dr. Gregory."

He was always serious, even when the sarcasm slipped out. Sophia Jackson was famous and frivolous and nothing more. She'd be in no danger if her name slipped out, but she didn't need to worry: Alex was not a man who let names slip. He could remember a time when his mother's life had depended on his ability to keep her name a secret.

He paused, mentally closing the door on unwelcome memories. "Every room is full because you've got only one doctor on duty, so let me get back to work. Sophia Jackson will survive with curtains instead of walls. I've already examined her, so there's nothing medical for anyone to overhear, anyway. If she doesn't want anyone to overhear her other types of complaints, then she can stop complaining."

"Yes, Doctor."

"Loretta, one more thing. When the soccer kid in room three goes for his X-ray, make sure he doesn't cross paths with Sophia Jackson. He's a big fan of one of her movies, and I don't—"

"You wouldn't want him to bother Miss Jackson."

"Actually, I wouldn't want Miss Jackson to ruin his image of her."

"Understood. By the way, her personal assistant is going to want to know how we'll keep her identity a secret while we roll her gurney down to radiology."

"If Miss Jackson doesn't want to be seen, then perhaps her personal assistant would care to throw a blanket over her head."

"I don't get paid enough to deliver that message."

Alex sighed. "I'll talk to her assistant myself."

Grace was very aware that a new patient had been placed on the other side of the curtain, a woman who'd barely answered the nurse's questions with more than a syllable. There was a man with her, too, who'd loudly done most of the talking. Now that the nurse had left them alone, he was keeping his voice to a vicious whisper, but Grace could still hear him.

She wished she couldn't.

"You already know what I'll do to you, bitch. You want to see what I'll do to your kids?"

Grace looked at Sophia in a panic, but she was lying on her bed, twisted away from her, typing madly away on the precious phone Grace had retrieved.

The unseen man on the other side of the curtain was obviously trying to be quiet, but he wasn't quiet enough for Grace's ears. "You tell the doctor you fell down the stairs. Say it. Now."

"I f-fell down the stairs," the woman said. "But we don't have stairs."

"The effing doctor doesn't know that, you dumb-ass."

Grace was paralyzed in her vinyl chair. She'd be horrified if this were a movie scene, but this was even worse. This was real life, and she was no Sophia Jackson heroine. Grace didn't know what to do.

"Say it again, like you mean it."

"I fell down the stairs."

"Smile when you say it. You get me in trouble, I will hunt your kids. You send me to jail, and they're dead when I get out."

Grace couldn't move. Couldn't make a noise. The man clearly didn't know someone was sitting inches behind him on the other side of a cloth curtain. If she made a sound, he would.

What would he do? Would he hurt those children that were apparently waiting somewhere in a one-story house?

Frantically, she reached forward to tap the mattress of her sister's gurney, but her sister only hunched her shoulders and kept tapping away on her screen.

"Don't worry," the woman said, sounding so pitiful as she tried to soothe the man who had hurt her, who was threatening her still. "Everything will be okay. You can trust me, you know you can. I would never want you to get in trouble. I'll fix everything."

On her gurney, Sophia coughed.

Grace froze.

There was utter silence on the other side of the curtain, and then the curtain was pushed aside. "Who the hell are you?"

She had to do something. Her sister's back was to the angry man, so before Sophia could roll over and reveal her famous face, Grace jumped to her feet and faced him. "We'd like some privacy." She dared to grab the curtain and whisk it shut, right in the man's face.

The silence on the other side of the curtain was more frightening than the angry whispers had been. Her heart was already pounding out of her chest when she heard more curtains being pushed aside on their metal rings. Not hers—the ones next door.

"Good afternoon, I'm Dr. Gregory. What brings you in today?"

"I fell down the stairs."

Her sister chose that moment to emerge from her absorption in the phone. "How slow is this place? Didn't you tell them to bring the X-ray machine up here?"

Frantically, Grace put her finger against her lips to silence Sophia. *Shh, shh, shh...*

"What is wrong with you?"

"Nothing." Grace leaned in close to her sister's ear, so she could whisper. "I want to hear what they're saying next door."

"What for?"

She cringed. Every normally spoken word sounded like a trumpet blast to Grace. She could hear the man doing most of the talking next door. The woman's voice sounded so timid. The third person, the one who'd said he was

Dr. Gregory, had a better voice. Calm and confident. He spoke with the good cheer of someone who didn't know his patient was in danger.

"We'll need a few X-rays because you might have one or more fractures. There's a bit of a wait for radiology right now."

Sophia spoke loudly. "This X-ray is taking forever."

Grace whirled around and pleaded for silence with her finger on her lips. It figured that Sophia had just now started paying attention.

Dr. Gregory kept talking. "While you're waiting, Mr. Burns, you can get the paperwork taken care of. You'll be able to leave sooner that way."

The curtain rings made their sliding sound again.

"Loretta, perfect timing. Could you show Mr. Burns to admin while we're waiting to take Mrs. Burns to X-ray? He needs to fill out the spousal consent forms."

"The spousal consent forms? If you'll just follow me, Mr. Burns."

After another swish of curtain rings, the violent Mr. Burns was gone with the nurse.

"We'll take care of you," Dr. Gregory said to the woman. "It might have sounded like I was rushing you out of here, but you can stay as long as you need to."

Grace held her breath, willing the woman to tell the doctor the truth while her attacker was gone. She heard only silence.

"I'll be back shortly." The doctor was leaving.

Grace needed to be brave. She should do something. Say something.

But she didn't. She was no superhero. Maybe she could write a note and pass it to a nurse or something…

Behind her, Sophia called out. "Dr. Gregory."

There was an audible sigh in the aisle. Then it was

their curtain that was being pushed aside, and a man far younger than Grace had expected stepped into their little space. He was around thirty, bespectacled and bearded. Not the trendy kind of full beard that men in Hollywood were wearing this year, but the dark shadow of a man who'd perhaps worked a twenty-four-hour shift.

"Yes, Miss Jackson?" He sounded as tired as he looked.

Sophia began complaining. The doctor listened to her sister's demands without a flicker of emotion on his face, without so much as a blink of his eyes behind his brown plastic eyeglass frames. His white overcoat looked too big on him. He didn't look like a man, frankly, who could handle the vicious Mr. Burns, but—

But, actually, he did.

There was something very Clark Kent about him. Tall, dark and handsome could have described him if he were in Superman mode, but as Clark Kent, he was too unassuming to be eye-catching, not the way he stood with his hands stuffed in the square pockets of his lab coat. Still, although he might not have bothered to shave, his jawline was defined, and the blue of his eyes was only dimmed a little bit by the glare of the fluorescent lighting on his eyeglasses.

It was the look in those blue eyes that gave Grace hope. He saw right through her sister. He wasn't flustered by her beauty and he didn't look awed to have a movie star in his presence. In fact, he was looking at her with quiet disapproval. If he could see through the celebrity aura that surrounded Sophia Jackson, maybe he could see through Mr. Burns. Grace just needed to be brave enough to tell him what she'd heard.

"So, um, you're her doctor?" she began, forcing herself to smile when it was the last thing on earth she wanted to do at the moment.

He turned that blue gaze directly on her. A small eternity of silence followed.

"Of course he is," Sophia said, exasperated. "I told him you'd fix everything when you got here. I need a private room. These curtains are so ghetto."

He didn't take his eyes off Grace, but he raised one dark brow behind the brown frames. "*You're* the personal assistant?"

Clearly, he wasn't impressed with her. She felt badly about that, another little dagger of hurt to push through. "Dr. Gregory, could I speak to you somewhere else? Somewhere private?"

"No."

Grace blinked. "I really need to speak to you alone."

"There are no other rooms available, and there is nothing you can say that will make radiology move more quickly. As soon as her X-rays are complete, you'll be discharged with treatment instructions, and you can seek out all the privacy you desire somewhere else."

He left.

Sophia's outrage drowned out Grace's disappointment. She yelled "Doctor" once more, but the doctor wasn't coming back.

Grace sank back into her chair, a failure.

"What do you think you're doing, Grace? Go after him." Sophia was loud for someone who prized her privacy. She gestured toward the ice packs on her leg. "I can't get up and walk out of here. You have to."

"He already said no."

"This whole trip was your idea. Go fix it. What's a personal assistant for, right?"

Chapter Four

Alex headed straight for the staff's kitchenette. There were patients to be seen, lab results to read, decisions to be made, but he was only one man. He needed a break—and coffee. Just three minutes, that was all he'd give himself. Three minutes for a little caffeine and a chance to regain his emotional equilibrium after dealing with Mr. Burns, the scum who'd beaten his wife.

Gut churning, Alex walked past the coffee to the cramped locker room that was attached to the kitchen. The room barely had enough space for a few metal lockers and a single cot, but the door had a small sign which euphemistically declared it to be the physician's lounge. He pushed a gym bag out of the way with his foot on his way to the sink. The water ran hot almost instantly.

The patient had not fallen down a flight of stairs, that much was obvious from her bruising. Alex had needed to pretend he believed her story, though. Abusers wouldn't stick around after an accusation, and they often convinced their victims to leave before they could be treated. Alex had started the hospital's official process, and he hoped the victim was ready to take advantage of the assistance the hospital could provide.

The system worked. He'd seen it work. But to use an American phrase, that first step was a doozy. The first step required Alex to smile and be cordial and shake hands with a man he was certain had beaten his own wife.

Alex scrubbed his hands in the sink. He was no actor, but he deserved an Academy Award for keeping up that facade of friendliness. To test his patience further, a real actor, Sophia Jackson, had decided to waste his time by chewing him out for problems that weren't even problems.

Alex scrubbed harder. Hot water, soap and vigorous friction could kill almost anything.

The woman on one side of the curtain had been a victim of a crime. Sophia Jackson, on the other side of the curtain, had been a victim of nothing more than her own stupidity and stubbornness. According to the Texas Rescue volunteers who'd brought her in, she'd decided to cut short a tour of the rebuilt clinic by storming off the path, stomping over the orange netting that marked off the rubble left behind by last year's floods. They'd called after her and warned her to stop, but the paramedic said she'd ignored everyone.

Alex could believe it. It seemed the movie star was nothing more than a miserable person who made everyone around her miserable, too. Her personal assistant looked to be the most unhappy person of them all.

He stopped scrubbing and let the tap water flow over his hands. The personal assistant hadn't been what he'd expected. Instead of a hard and edgy shark, she looked like an angel. The expression on her heart-shaped face was open and hopeful. Everything about her had seemed inviting. Her hair looked soft and touchable, a shade of gold so dark, it was nearly bronze. The overhead lighting had reflected off that gold, and Alex had been momentarily dazzled by her halo before he'd realized who she was. Only then had he noticed the subtle, anxious way she was twisting her fingers together.

Apparently, even an angel could be stressed out. It would take the patience of a saint to work for Sophia Jackson.

He used a paper towel to shut off the faucet. If the angelic woman was stressed out by the demands of Sophia Jackson, he couldn't help her. Since she was with the movie star, he could only assume that she enjoyed her job. Fame was alluring to most people, perhaps even more so to personal assistants. After all, they made a living by helping someone famous keep their famous life running smoothly. Princess Picasso's assistant was no exception.

He grabbed a coffee mug, feeling annoyed with himself for being annoyed at all. It shouldn't matter to him one bit that an angelic-looking woman who happened to pass through his ER was letting a movie star run her ragged. It was no business of his whether or not she thrived by facilitating someone's fame. Coffee was all he wanted.

The door opened after the most timid of knocks. "Excuse me, Dr. Gregory. I'm so sorry to bother you." The assistant stuck her angel face in the crack and smiled at him hopefully.

Speak of the devil.

"This area is employees only."

She bit her lower lip with perfect white teeth. "I know, I'm sorry."

He set down the empty mug. So, she was appealing. They had nothing in common and would never see each

other again after another sixty minutes, give or take, so he
called upon his medical experience to act dispassionately
and moved to the door.

"I really need to talk to you," she said.

"There is nothing you can say that will change how this
hospital operates."

You stay in your world, I'll stay in mine. He put his hand
on the doorknob to shut it.

"Wait." The angel had more determination than he'd
expected. She thrust her whole arm and shoulder in the
door. "There are no stairs in her house."

He knew, instantly, that she was not telling him about
Sophia Jackson's house. Surprise kept him silent.

"I heard her say so. I'm talking about the woman next to
us. The man that was with her hurt her." She was breathless in her anxiety to tell him what she knew.

Alex opened the door and ushered her in with a gentle
touch on her arm, a brief brush of her soft gray sweater
under his hand. He shut the door in an automatic move to
protect patient privacy. Still, it seemed intimate to be alone
with this woman in this little bit of an inner sanctum. "I
understand. That's why I arranged to have him removed
from her treatment area."

She didn't seem reassured. "He's only filling out paperwork. Spousal consent forms."

She really had heard every word, then—and remembered them. "Spousal consent forms are a code in this ER.
It means the spouse has to leave the treatment area. I've
seen enough patients who have fallen down stairs to recognize the hallmarks of that type of injury."

"And she didn't have them?"

He shook his head silently. He was bound legally and
ethically not to describe a patient's medical condition to

a stranger. The assistant obviously knew some details already, but he couldn't tell her more.

"How long does it take for him to fill out the forms? He'll be back any minute."

"Security will explain that he can't reenter the treatment area. Doctor's orders. When the next room with walls and a door opens up, the patient will be moved there. I can't tell you more than that, but I assure you, she will have a chance to talk to me in private."

"She won't tell you anything."

Sadly, the assistant was quite possibly right. Victims of domestic violence were often silent in the hope that the situation would improve if they helped their abuser. "I hope you're wrong about that, but we'll give her every chance, every safety net we have available. You and I need to end this conversation now, because—"

Because of patient confidentiality, of course. But he didn't finish the sentence, because what had popped into his head was *because you're already too appealing.* Her compassion toward a stranger only increased his regard for her.

It didn't matter. He had no interest in pursuing a woman when no relationship was possible. Flirting was something else he'd never quite understood. It was a waste of time to indulge an attraction to a woman who lived in another state, let alone a woman who built her life on the shaky ground of fame.

The assistant furrowed her brow, determination stamped on her lovely face. "You can get her alone in a private room, but she won't tell you anything. She has children. He told her he would kill them if she talks."

The kitchenette door started to open beside them. He stopped it with the palm of his hand. "A moment, please." Without looking to see who it was, he pushed the door shut.

All his attention was for the assistant. "You heard this? He actually said he'd kill her children?"

"He was inches away from me on the other side of that curtain. I heard every word. He said if he goes to jail, he'll kill the children as soon as he gets out."

She looked up at him with fear and worry—and something else. Hope. She was looking at him as if she hoped he would be able to fix this terrible situation. The desire to touch her again, to physically soothe her, was completely inappropriate. That wasn't how a doctor helped.

He crossed his arms over his chest. "Are you willing to relay this to the police?"

"I hadn't thought about police."

This protective streak was strong. He didn't want her involved in what could become a volatile situation. "The injuries are already enough to trigger social services, and that will include removing the children from his custody. I appreciate everything you've told me, but you don't have to do anything else."

"No, I'll talk to the police. That poor woman. I couldn't live with myself if I didn't try to help."

"Not everyone feels the same. You're very brave." He felt a little sloppy bit of tenderness toward her, despite the way he was standing with his arms crossed over his chest, scowling at her. He cleared his throat and tried for a more neutral expression. "What did you say your name was?"

"It's Grace."

"Grace." Of course it was. Grace was a blessing one did nothing to deserve, *milost'* in his mother's language. He'd done nothing to merit its presence in his emergency department today, but Grace was here, being an ally for a stranger in a dangerous situation.

She tugged the hem of her soft sweater an inch lower. "Well, thanks for your time."

A brave princess had shown up in his ER after all—just not the one he'd expected.

He liked this one much better. "Thank you for being so persistent. I apologize for being so curt. I can tell you're worried, but you've done the right thing. I'll take it from here."

"What about the police?"

"If they need your statement, we'll do that with as much privacy as possible, I promise. I don't want you to risk anything if you don't have to."

"Thank you."

Grace left, slipping easily around the nurse who was waiting outside the door.

"Loretta asked me to tell you that we're taking Mrs. Burns down to X-ray now. Room three is ready to go, if you could discharge him. The social worker is on her way over."

Alex would have to get his coffee later. As he headed down the hall toward room three, Grace was about twenty feet ahead of him on her way back to the curtained area. Her plain clothing allowed him to enjoy the feminine shape of her. He knew firsthand that her sweater felt very soft, and her slacks were tailored over the curve of her backside.

The voice of Princess Picasso came shrieking down the hall. "You have got to be kidding me! Why is that woman getting an X-ray before me?"

Grace broke into a jog.

Alex shook his head as he entered room three. How could an angel who was so brave subject herself to a celebrity who was so selfish?

"Here's your macchiato." Grace hiked her tote bag a little higher on her shoulder and held up the cup of coffee she'd spent fifteen minutes locating, ordering, paying for and bringing to her sister.

Sophia was talking on her phone, and waved her into silence. The part-skim half-caff macchiato with the shot of regular caramel syrup and sugar-free vanilla syrup which she'd just *had* to have was not quite as important as her phone call, apparently.

Grace was tempted to place it on the bedside table and leave the table where it was, at the foot of the bed. Sophia would need her then. She'd have to interrupt her phone call with Deezee to ask Grace to roll the table closer.

Immediately, Grace admonished herself for being such a baby. What kind of sister would even think of placing something where a person with a broken leg couldn't reach it?

"You asked to see me?" Dr. Gregory entered their little curtained cubicle and stood at the foot of Sophia's gurney, next to Grace.

Grace put the coffee down. She wasn't normally klutzy, but she felt a little flutter now that Dr. Gregory was here, so it was better not to be holding a scalding-hot beverage.

Really, she needed to squelch this little Clark Kent crush. The man was on the job, caring for a battered woman somewhere else. Caring for her own injured sister, too, and who knew how many other people who were sick and in pain. Yet she felt a little buzz of excitement that he was here, despite knowing that her sister shouldn't have demanded to see him.

"The doctor decided to finally show up," Sophia said into her phone. "Yeah, tell me about it."

Grace stole a glance at Dr. Gregory. He pushed his glasses up with one knuckle. He had a perfectly neutral poker face in place, but Grace had the fanciful thought that the move meant he was ready for battle.

Sophia took the phone away from her ear and pointed it at the doctor accusingly. "I heard them talking next door. You know what they said?"

Grace held her breath. What had she missed while she'd been looking for gourmet coffee? The horrible Mr. Burns must have returned. Or perhaps Mrs. Burns had decided to unburden herself to a nurse, and Sophia had overheard everything.

"Your janitor told another janitor to take the patient's belongings to room three. That patient is getting a room? Seriously? When I've been waiting here with nothing but curtains all this time?"

Grace interceded before Sophia could make a fool of herself. "Sophia, it's okay."

"No, it is not. I was here first. She got taken for an X-ray before me, and now she gets a goddamned room before me."

"Sophie," Grace begged quietly. "The cursing."

"*Goddamn* won't even get you a PG-13 rating." Sophie pinned the doctor with her glare. Really, it was a sneer. Grace hated to see Sophie sneering like that. If she could take a photo, make Sophie see...

"I demand a private room, for obvious reasons."

"There are none available." Dr. Gregory didn't sound upset or intimidated by Sophia's behavior at all, not like Grace was.

Sophia must have heard that almost bored note in his voice, too, because she hesitated, just for a second, in the middle of ramping herself up for a good old-fashioned hissy fit. She gave it a go, anyway. "Even if I didn't need extra privacy, which you know I do, I should have been next. I've been waiting longer."

"That's not the way it works in a hospital. She needs the room more than you do, and there are patients who require my presence right now more than you do." He stepped back and grabbed the curtain, ready to leave. "Was there anything else?"

"More than I do?" Sophia's voice was getting high-pitched in her outrage. "I suppose you decide that?"

"I do."

Grace felt a little chill go down her spine at the quiet confidence in those words. She looked at Dr. Gregory again, at his calm profile, his unwavering gaze.

He can handle anything. He can handle Mr. Burns. He can handle my sister.

Then she realized he'd turned to her, locking gazes with her for the briefest of moments, just long enough for her to imagine he was silently asking her to keep Sophia under control.

I wish I could.

"You're just leaving?" Sophia sounded incredulous.

Grace wished she had as much control over her sister as Dr. Gregory seemed to think she had. She put a hand on her sister's good ankle and patted her reassuringly. "Thank you, Dr. Gregory. We'll stay right here, then, until a room opens up."

He nodded at her. "I'll be back."

Grace hoped he'd be quick. His hair was shaggy and he needed to shave—yesterday—and his glasses weren't chic geek, just geek. His white coat was two sizes too big, and yet he looked like a hero to her. Somehow, when Grace stood next to Dr. Gregory, Sophia seemed less intimidating, but he was gone with a slide of metal curtain rings, and Grace was left to manage her own personal movie star.

"Where the hell is that macchiato?"

Hurry back, Doctor. I need you.

Chapter Five

Grace wanted Dr. Gregory.

What she got was a frighteningly competent nurse named Loretta. The nurse seemed to be just as unimpressed with having a movie star for a patient as Dr. Gregory was, but still...

It would have been nicer to have Dr. Gregory by her side.

Sophia's ankle was not broken, the nurse reported, but she would need to wear a hard plastic medical boot for a week. The nurse removed the ice. She'd brought a few sizes of the plastic boot to try. By the time the correct boot was strapped around Sophia's lower leg, poor Sophia was clutching Grace's hand in real pain.

Nurse Loretta gave Sophia a pill for the pain, something Dr. Gregory had apparently foreseen the need to prescribe, then Grace and Sophia were alone again. This time, Grace perched on the edge of the bed, and they did yoga breaths together while they waited for the pain medicine to kick in.

"We could do 'breath of lion,'" Grace suggested.

"The dumb one where we stick out our tongues?" But Sophia made a funny face at Grace as she said it, one that always made Grace laugh. "Hope no one with a camera sees us."

The sarcasm, the cursing, the defiance had all disappeared in the last half hour. Grace stuck her tongue out and panted. Sophia did, too, but they couldn't keep panting with straight faces.

"Ohmigod, we look dorky," Sophia said, and the sound of her laughter was music to Grace's ears.

My sister is back.

Grace could have cried in relief. It was so good to be needed again—no, not needed. She was always needed. It was good to be wanted again. Sophia wanted her by her side.

Sophia's laugh turned into another round of coughing. Grace winced in sympathy; her sister's ribs had to hurt from the force of her cough. Sophia sank back into her pillow. She'd never looked more pitiful, not even on screen when she'd died as a pioneer woman to great critical acclaim.

Grace smoothed Sophie's hair over her shoulder. "Can I get you anything?"

She attempted another smile, a wobbly bit of bravery. "Just don't leave me again. I need you here."

"Of course."

I wish Dr. Gregory could see us now. He hadn't been very impressed with Sophia so far, that much was clear. When she'd complained about Mrs. Burns moving to a room, Dr. Gregory had thrown Grace that last look, the one that said *Can't you keep her in line?*

It nagged at Grace. Maybe the look had been more like *How do you put up with her?* Maybe the look had been simply disappointment with Grace. Or puzzlement. *Why do you help someone who is so rude?*

Because I love her. She's my sister. She's my whole family.

But, of course, Dr. Gregory didn't know that, just as Sophia didn't know anything about Mrs. Burns's dangerous situation. If she did, then of course she'd be content to wait a little longer. With a crinkle of the plastic-covered mattress under her, Grace scooted closer to her sister's side, ready to confide in her.

"Ouch! Don't bump me. Sit on that stool."

"Sorry." Grace slipped from the mattress onto the doctor's rolling stool, trying not to feel sad at how short-lived their shared laughter had been.

It wasn't Sophia's fault. She was still in pain, and the pain was making her irritable. Really, she was acting as normally as anyone would in her condition.

Grace leaned closer, too aware of the curtains, although no other patients were around now. "Listen, something kind of scary happened while you were on the phone with Deezee. The lady that was in the next bed—"

"The one who got treated better than I did?"

"I don't know about better. Maybe faster, but there was a good reason. Let me tell you what happened."

Mrs. Burns's sad tale had exactly the effect that Grace had known it would. Sophia was subdued, silent. Probably, like Grace, she was thinking how fortunate she was to have been born into a loving home, where the concept of Daddy hitting Mommy was unimaginable. This afternoon was a vivid reminder that other children were not so lucky.

"Then I'm glad they moved her," Sophia said.

"I know. Me, too."

"That would have been a mess, if the two of them had started fighting again. People would have come running, and these curtains wouldn't have kept us hidden. Hell, the guy could have thrown her right into our cubicle or something. I can't be involved in that kind of thing. Can you imagine the shock on everyone's faces if the curtain had come down and they'd seen Sophia Jackson lying here?"

Grace was silent. That wasn't exactly the empathy she'd expected.

"Martina is threatening to leave me if I'm involved in any fights," Sophia said. "She told Deezee the same thing."

Martina was a publicist, and one of the few people whom Sophia still seemed to listen to. Then again, Martina had been Deezee's publicist first. She'd introduced the two of them, actually. It was yet another reason that Grace doubted Deezee had any real affection for Sophia. She'd been awfully good for improving his damaged reputation. He'd had the opposite effect on hers—so now Martina was helping Sophia, too, for a hefty retainer fee.

Sophia let go of her hand and pushed herself into more of a sitting position. Her pain was clearly lessening. The medicine must be kicking in. "What time is our flight? I'm ready to get out of here."

I'm not.

Grace wanted to stay here, where Deezee and publicists had no importance. Here, someone else was in charge.

The curtain rings slid open, and Dr. Gregory walked in, laptop under his arm. Intelligent, empathetic, authoritative—Grace wanted to run to him and cling to his hand.

She stood up to let him have his rolling stool, but he waved her back down and took the straight chair on the opposite side of the bed. When he asked Sophia how her ankle was feeling in the boot, he seemed genuinely interested in what she had to say. His bedside manner, when he was literally bedside, was sympathetic and focused on the patient.

Then again, what man didn't focus on Sophia Jackson? The two of them looked quite striking together. Maybe not at a glance—Sophia had on that killer coat dress and her hair still looked fabulous after a couple of hours in a hospital bed, while Dr. Gregory was kind of lost under his baggy coat and shaggy hair—but they both had vividly blue eyes and really great bone structure. They'd make beautiful babies together. Beautiful, intelligent, talented babies.

Another stab to her chest caught her by surprise. Jealousy? She couldn't be jealous of the attention Sophia was paying to Dr. Gregory. The idea of Dr. Gregory and Sophia together ought to make her happy.

"The ankle will heal, as long as you don't push it too soon. That's the good news."

"There's bad news?" Sophia asked, half playful, half fearful. Clearly, she'd decided to try being charming and pleasant. She was succeeding.

Dr. Gregory opened his laptop. "Let's look at that chest X-ray."

Grace's heart squeezed again at the sight of their two heads leaning over the computer screen together. The good news? He'd make a wonderful brother-in-law. The bad news? Her sister was too shallow to look past the surface to see what a quality guy the doctor was.

I can see it.

Yes, but you aren't the one who needs to see it.

Grace snapped out of her conversation with herself. Chest X-ray? Sophia hadn't mentioned that she'd gotten her chest X-rayed along with her ankle.

"I have pneumonia?" Sophia sounded very skeptical, but she was looking at Dr. Gregory in a whole new way, like maybe he did know something she didn't know, after all.

Dr. Gregory smiled kindly at her, an appealing little crinkle of the corners of his eyes behind unattractive brown frames. "Walking pneumonia is the common term, because younger adults tend to get this particular kind, and they keep gutting it out and going to work despite feeling sick."

Oh, Sophia liked that implication that she was a trooper, Grace could tell. The show must go on, and all that jazz. Sophia relaxed back on her pillows a little bit.

"See this cloudy part of your lung? That's fluid accumulating in a place air should be. I could've diagnosed pneumonia on your lung sounds alone, to be honest, but since you were going into X-ray anyway, it was best to have your lungs checked out."

For weeks, Grace hadn't been able to persuade Sophia to take care of that cough, but Dr. Gregory had been able to do something about it. Still, Grace was astounded at the pneumonia diagnosis. She'd thought the cough was bad, but she hadn't expected it to be that bad.

"How long have you been coughing?" Dr. Gregory asked.

Sophia looked to Grace, the keeper of all mundane information. "How long? A couple weeks?"

Dr. Gregory looked at Grace, as well, waiting for her answer.

Grace felt that little flutter again that came with having his attention on her. "At least a month. It started shortly after…after we got back from Vegas." She'd been about to say *shortly after you and Deezee were caught in the police raid on that club*, but she didn't want to remind Sophia of something that would make her feel bad. Sophia had apologized for that already. Besides, she was finally showing her good side to Dr. Gregory, and Grace wanted him to see that her sister was a good person.

"I had pneumonia for a month and didn't know it?"

"I imagine you've felt worn-out every day," Dr. Gregory said, his attention back on Sophia.

Sophia nodded, managing to look like a martyr without looking overly dramatic at all. She was a great actress.

"But you've kept working anyway?" he asked.

Another nod.

Grace should have felt her usual amusement at how Sophia could have anyone eating out of her hand. Instead, she felt a little irritated. Sophia had been working only if one counted clubbing as work. The pile of scripts that represented future work kept stacking up, because Sophia had been too tired to evaluate new projects after running around with her boyfriend. Today's clinic opening had been the first actual work Sophia had done in weeks, and she'd tried to cut that short.

She had a good reason for that. She must have felt awful. She's really sick. What kind of sister am I to hold it against her?

Dr. Gregory nodded at Sophia in what surely looked like approval. "You need to take a break, starting today. Pneumonia won't go away by itself. I'm going to discharge you with some antibiotics. You'll want to see your own physician once you finish the medicine to be certain your lungs are clear, but in the meantime, you need to rest. Drink more fluids than you want to, and don't skip any pills, even once you start feeling better."

Discharge her? He was sending them away with some pills and a plastic boot? Grace felt a little panic. She didn't want to start negotiating an airport with a sick sister in a wheelchair. Her sister had laughed with her a few minutes ago. She was being positively pleasant to Dr. Gregory now. Texas was good for her. They needed to stay right here.

"You shouldn't fly again until we've had a chance to clear up some of this fluid in your lungs," Dr. Gregory said.

Yes! The man was a miracle. Forget clinging to his hand. Grace wanted to throw her arms around him.

Sophia's radiance dimmed. "I have to get back to LA right away."

"Even in a pressurized cabin on a commercial airliner, the demand on the lungs increases. This fluid is making things difficult enough for you here on the ground. How did you feel on the flight here?"

"Ohmigod, I felt terrible, actually. I was so tired and I had such a headache. I thought it was just a crappy flight."

You thought it was all my fault, like I'd booked a flight just to torture you.

"You probably weren't getting enough oxygen." Dr. Gregory closed the laptop. "Low oxygen saturation can cause those symptoms and more. Irritability, confusion and eventually loss of consciousness."

"Irritability?" Grace repeated without thinking.

To Grace's surprise, Sophia held her hand out to her. "Oh, Grace, I really took it out on you during the flight, didn't I? I said some mean things. I'm sorry."

Grace took her hand. Squeezed. This was the second time she'd gotten to see the nice side of her sister again— and Dr. Gregory was here to see it, too. Maybe now he wouldn't give her that puzzled look. This was proof that she didn't work for an uncontrollable diva. The longer they stayed in Texas, the more like her old self her sister became.

"We didn't know I had pneumonia, though, did we? I'll make it up to you. I promise to be extra nice to you on the plane tonight. It won't happen again."

"No, it won't," Dr. Gregory said firmly. "You can't fly tonight. Your ankle injury is taxing your body more than you might think. Between that stress and the pneumonia, you'd almost certainly be oxygen deprived again."

Sophia blinked at him. "But you can give me something for that, can't you?"

"For oxygen deprivation?" One corner of Dr. Gregory's mouth quirked upward. "Sure. It's called oxygen. You carry a tank of it with you and stick tubes up your nostrils so you don't pass out at thirty thousand feet and force an emergency landing."

Sophia's hand slid out of Grace's to land on the blankets with a little plop. Grace looked closely at Dr. Gregory. His poker face was good, but Grace could have sworn he was getting some satisfaction out of setting Sophia straight.

He stood and tucked the laptop under his arm. "Carrying an oxygen tank aboard would require some planning with the airline in advance. It's only allowed when the patient absolutely must travel. I'm not going to authorize it. Your ankle needs to stay immobilized and elevated, as well. I'll write a medical excuse for you, so the airline won't charge you to reschedule today's flight."

Double yes. Grace wanted to pump a fist in the air in victory. He couldn't have been more crystal clear. They were grounded, stuck in Texas. Who needed Superman when Clark Kent was doing the job so perfectly? Oh, God—was she smiling?

Grace bit her lip. Karma was surely going to get her. She'd wanted to get away from LA and stay away, and now Sophia was both injured and ill—but neither too seriously. Perfect.

Yikes. She was such a bad sister. To assuage her guilt, she pulled out a notebook from her trusty tote bag and started a new list. Flights would have to be changed. The hotel would have to be extended. She'd ask the concierge at their Hollywood condominium to hold the mail, or possibly deliver it here, depending on the length of their stay.

She looked up from her notebook. "How long are we staying here, then?"

"You should give the antibiotics a week. When she's breathing easier and her cough is better, you can fly."

"A week?" Sophia closed her eyes and pressed her fingertips to her forehead, overplaying her role a bit, in Grace's opinion.

"It could take you a month or more to feel a hundred percent back to normal, so don't be surprised if the fatigue continues on well past a week."

"A month?" Grace couldn't keep the happy anticipation out of her voice as she flipped to a fresh page in her notebook. "Oh, Sophie. I'll find us a real house, a vacation rental for a month. I'll get our clothes sent here, and line up some grocery service, and—"

"No." Sophia opened her eyes and glared at her from under her fingers. "I already told you I didn't want to stay an extra day. I won't be able to stand a week. Don't make one of your damned lists for anything except getting me back to LA."

Grace pretended she couldn't feel the disapproval Dr. Gregory was sending her sister's way. "We don't have a choice, Sophie. It will be good for you. You've been burning the candle at both ends."

Sophia snapped her fingers. "Book Deezee a flight. He can come out here and keep me company."

No, no, no!

"There's plenty of room in our suite."

It would be a nightmare. There'd be bottles of tequila everywhere, a man who referred to women as his *bitches* ordering Grace to fetch food and find limos for the strangers he'd invite up to their suite. There'd be noise complaints and hotel security and charges assessed for property damage. Grace would be scrambling around the clock. She couldn't take it, she just couldn't do it.

Dr. Gregory, she realized, was watching her intently.

Her hand was shaking. She pressed the pencil into the notebook to steady it, so it wouldn't give her away. If she got angry, if she said no, Sophia would be dead set on yes. She needed a new tactic. Quick.

The tip of the pencil broke, a little black scribble on her paper.

"Grace," the doctor said, "could I speak—"

"Isn't pneumonia contagious?" She tried not to sound desperate.

His easy bedside manner was gone, but his stilted answer was still courteous. "Pneumonia isn't contagious, but the bacterium that causes it is. Someone who comes in contact with her might develop any type of infection from it. Sinusitis, bronchitis. Those could lead to pneumonia."

"Are you kidding me?" But whatever else Sophia had been about to say was lost in a coughing jag.

Grace brushed the broken pencil lead off her notebook page. She could leverage this. She could tell Deezee that Sophia was contagious, although he was as bad as Sophia, doing the opposite of anything Grace suggested. She could tell their publicist. Sophia and Deezee both listened to Martina...

"Grace, could I speak to you for a minute?" Dr. Gregory asked.

She looked up at him. He was much taller than she was, so she'd been looking up at him all afternoon, but he seemed like a giant now as she sat in the chair. "Of course."

"What for?" Sophia croaked, not quite done with her cough.

"Alone?" he added.

Sophia grabbed Grace's arm, making the pencil drag across the page. "You said you wouldn't leave me again."

Sophia looked so genuinely distressed, Grace didn't have the heart to point out that she'd left her to fetch the cell phone and left to fetch the caramel non-van half-caff macchiato because Sophia had ordered her to. Right now, she looked like a little puppy that needed protecting.

Grace looked from her sister's blue eyes up to Dr. Gregory's. He seemed so solid, so calm. He had the authority to deny air travel, to order medical tests, even to protect a woman from an abusive spouse.

He could help her.

She stood. "Don't worry, Sophie. I'll be back in a minute."

With a slide of metal curtain rings, she left with Dr. Gregory.

Chapter Six

Alex was dazzled by the sight of Grace in the bright Texas sun.

Being dazzled was, of course, the temporary effect of walking from the windowless emergency room into the bright sunlight of the ambulance bay. *Light adaptation* was the medical term. He watched Grace blink, a reflexive move to relieve the visual discomfort as the retinas chemically altered to favor cones over rods.

Or maybe she was just a pretty girl, shading her eyes on a sunny spring afternoon, and he was just a guy who wanted to get to know her better.

Life was only that simple in Hollywood movies.

Alex's life had never been charmed. He was starting to suspect this woman's life wasn't quite the American dream it appeared to be on the surface, either.

He couldn't grill her about her apparent anxiety when it came to Sophia Jackson. As he had with his young soccer-playing patient, he started with something that he knew wouldn't cause pain. "I wanted to let you know that Mrs. Burns has decided to use the services we offered her. She's got an advocate with her now who will escort her to a women's shelter when she's ready to leave."

"That's wonderful." Grace's smile dazzled him in a way that had nothing to do with the chemistry of the retinas. The fine tension she carried in her shoulders eased a fraction. With a firm touch, he could eliminate the rest, smoothing his thumbs from insertion to origin point on each tight muscle.

Alex put his hands in the pockets of his white coat.

"And the children?" Grace asked. "What happens to them?"

"They'll be picked up and brought to the safe house with their mother."

"That is really, really good news. Thank you so much for telling me."

"Of course."

He realized he was staring into her eyes —warm and brown and gold, like her hair—when she looked away. Just how long had that silent bit of gazing between them lasted?

She made a gesture, a small wave at nothing in particular. An equally delicate worry line appeared between her brows. "Are you going to get in trouble for breaking a privacy rule or something? Is that why you brought me outside?"

"No. You volunteered to be a witness if necessary. It's reasonable for me to let you know that the patient is speaking up for herself, so you don't have to."

Her compassion extended to him, then. She was kind to worry that he'd be in trouble. Maybe she was too compassionate, though. If she didn't guard her heart, she would always be worrying about others.

She smiled again, another bit of tension leaving her shoulders. "I'm so glad to hear that. Can you keep me updated? I want to know if everything turns out okay."

"That probably would be crossing a line when it comes to privacy laws. I doubt I'll ever get an update, either. I don't see most of my patients more than once."

That little frown of worry appeared again. "You don't get to find out how your patients are doing?"

"Not often. I do my best while they're here and discharge them with instructions and prescriptions and referrals. Whether they use them or not is up to them."

She touched him. There was no purpose to it, not like there was when he touched someone. She just laid her hand on his arm, not pressing, not squeezing, not demanding. "You must be a very special kind of person, then. I couldn't do your job. I'd go crazy wondering how everyone is."

He'd brought her out here because he was concerned about her anxiety, the hand wringing and the pencil breaking. If she worried for the whole world like this, then he supposed she must always need an outlet for her emotions. He hadn't meant to add himself to her list of people to worry about.

He'd been on his feet for hours, and he was ready for a break. The unexpected influx of afternoon patients was under control. He could take a few minutes now, with her. He nodded toward the empty metal bench that was usually occupied by a paramedic or firefighter whose emergency vehicle was parked outside the ER's portico.

The curved steel of the bench couldn't have felt better after hours of standing. The woman by his side couldn't have been more beautiful to look at. The sun was shining, the weather was perfect...

Life was never that simple. He'd brought her out here for a reason. Something about her relationship with Sophia

Jackson was setting off his suspicions. *I'm sorry for being mean to you* her boss had said to her, but of course, Jackson had almost immediately excused her own bad behavior by bringing up the pneumonia. *It won't happen again. I'll make it up to you.* How many times had a woman with a black eye heard that from the man who'd hurt her?

He doubted Sophia Jackson physically hurt Grace, but she was still pulling some emotionally manipulative stunts. Why did Grace put up with it? There had to be other jobs, other people she could work for. He'd brought her outside because he was concerned about all these things, but now she was concerned for him.

"Don't all these people weigh on your mind? How do you handle the not knowing?"

Maybe she was hoping he'd give her some advice on controlling worry. He rubbed his jaw and looked past a red ambulance to focus on a green cypress tree. The solitary evergreen pillar thrived in its allotted space in a median strip, surrounded by the concrete of the hospital parking lot. "I've found it helps if you choose their fate. Use your imagination. I helped a little girl with significant respiratory distress yesterday. I did everything I could to educate her family about asthma triggers. Today, I wondered if that family filled their script for the asthma inhalers. Did they stop smoking for her sake?" He fell silent, knowing the odds that smokers faced. Nicotine was as addicting as narcotics.

Grace prompted him with her gentle voice. "And you decided yes, the parents must have done the right thing and given up smoking?"

"I'm not so vain to think I can convince people to give up a lifelong addiction with one conversation." He glanced at her face, at her hopeful expression. "But I decided I was good enough at my job to persuade that family to never again smoke while that child is in the car with them. That's something."

"You're an optimist, then. I wouldn't have guessed that was hidden behind your—those—ah, never mind."

"Behind my what?"

She was blushing and utterly charming to him. She made a little gesture toward his face and shrugged.

"Behind my glasses? Are you afraid I'm insulted by that? I know I have glasses on." He took off his glasses. "Contacts are tough when shifts run into the next day without warning."

He looked at her as he wiped the lenses with a corner of his white coat, and thought the softer focus suited her.

Grace blinked again. Adapting to what? Surely her chemistry had settled down.

She cleared her throat. "I was going to say I didn't think you were an optimist behind that poker face. You don't give much away when you're in there, being a doctor."

He put his glasses back on, sliding them into place with one knuckle. He hoped his poker face didn't slip. He wasn't an optimist at all, but he didn't want to add to Grace's apparent worries. He couldn't tell her about the patients whose fates he did learn, the little girls who returned to the ER with blue lips, gasping for air, smelling like the cigarettes their families still smoked around them, triggering their asthma attacks for which the inhaler prescription had never been filled. Reality was too often bitter. It made a man hard.

An optimist wouldn't meet a movie star and assume her personal assistant was somehow trapped by her.

"When I discharge Sophia Jackson, what kind of living situation will she be in?" It was a legitimate question, one he asked every patient to be sure they could follow their treatment plan. What he really wanted to know was

Grace's living arrangements. He had no professional justification for investigating this. He was just…

Abusing my position to satisfy an unhealthy curiosity about this woman?

It didn't matter. He wanted to know that Grace was going to be okay when she walked out of the ER and out of his life. He wanted to be able to imagine a better fate for her than fetching and carrying for a diva, having her self-esteem chipped away with each selfish demand.

"Will you be with her, or will Miss Jackson be living alone?"

Grace seemed to sink a little bit, without slouching or changing her posture at all. "I'm her personal assistant. Where she goes, I go."

"Even at night? You live together?"

At Grace's nod, he felt a distinct disappointment. It was almost like finding out she belonged to another man. Spoken for. Unavailable.

Again, he was annoyed with himself. It was absurd to be disappointed that all her time was devoted to another person. It wasn't like he'd intended to ask her out for dinner.

He needed to behave like a doctor. "It's good that she won't be alone, because she's going to have a hard time getting around. Even with the hard boot, she won't be able to touch her foot to the ground without pain for at least twenty-four hours. She'll need assistance getting in and out of the shower, for example. Do you feel comfortable giving her that kind of aid? If not, I can write orders for a visiting nurse who can help her with personal care."

Grace turned her face away, looking as he had toward the distant cypress tree. "She taught me how to brush my teeth. We've been sharing a bathroom our whole lives. Sophia Jackson is my sister."

Family.

All the pieces fell into place. A bright angel, subjecting herself to servitude. A movie star, bossing around a valuable employee without fear that she'd quit. Sisters... Of course.

I really took it out on you. It won't happen again.

No one could hurt you like family could hurt you.

Papa. Mama.

He firmly pushed the memories back where they belonged.

There were no bruises on Grace. Her sister might be using the same soundtrack that most abusers used, but Grace wasn't *physically* scared of her sister. When it came to emotional manipulation, Alex was too pragmatic to believe he could help her unravel any knots of family power struggles, not during a five-minute break on a metal bench. His own family was so fractured, he had no advice to give.

As for his attraction to her, it was irrelevant. She lived in Hollywood; he lived in Texas. She chased fame; he helped the injured. There was no reason for him to invest energy and effort when there was no possibility of a lasting relationship.

But he wouldn't let his moment with Grace end yet. He needed to find out what she was going back to—what his patient was going back to, as well—what was behind the white lips and broken pencil when the name Deezee was mentioned. Sophia might not be hurting her sister, but someone named Deezee could be.

Who was he, and why was Grace scared of him?

Dr. Gregory had fallen silent next to her.

Grace had said she'd help her sister in and out of the shower, and now he had nothing to say. Perhaps he'd been struck speechless at the image of Sophia Jackson in the shower. That was pretty typical of most guys. He didn't have a smile on his face, though, not even the ghost of a smirk.

Grace had also told him she was Sophia's sister. She resigned herself to the more likely possibility that he was quiet while he, like everyone else, studied her face, looking for the resemblance. *Sisters? I never would have guessed.*

Being told she didn't look like her own sister was a fairly new phenomenon in the overall course of her life. As little girls, they'd worn matching dresses and been declared darling. Even during her first two years of high school, every time she'd had a teacher that Sophia had already had, Grace had been told how she looked so much like her sister. It was only the stardom of the last few years that had begun separating them.

Sophia had acquired the polish and appearance of a star, that indefinable something that made people do a double take. Some of it was professional makeup, professional hair, and hours and hours of professional fitness training. Yet even without those things, Sophia still had a wow factor that Grace just didn't have. Sophia had been born with that charisma. She'd also been in the drama club, taken theater classes in college and developed a stage presence, but some gifts couldn't be taught, and Grace had always been proud to have such a gifted sister.

She was still proud of Sophia. This was only a phase. Grace just had to get Deezee out of their lives. Would Sophia ever consider Clark Kent?

Maybe, if they stayed away from LA long enough. Maybe, but no one could fall in love with someone they only met once. Grace needed to arrange more time between Dr. Gregory and Sophia.

"We're at the Hotel Houston," she said, before she could chicken out. "In Austin. It's called Houston, but it's not far from here."

"I know it. Very nice. I'm sure the concierge will help you get some chicken soup for your sister. Hot beverages and hot, steamy showers will help loosen up the debris in her lungs."

Back to the shower fantasy, then. Grace felt glum about that, although it boded well for the hope that he might become a future brother-in-law. But Sophia wouldn't give the doctor or anyone else a chance, not if Grace couldn't keep Deezee away. "And she's contagious, and definitely can't be around other people right now, right?"

"That's the second time you've asked that. Are you afraid you'll catch something, or are you afraid of someone else?"

A little shiver threatened to go down her spine. He was looking at her so intently as he asked.

"Afraid? I guess I should be. Sophia Jackson causing an epidemic would be a terrible headline to try to spin." Grace sighed, realizing her plan to replace Deezee with this serious man was a laughably long shot. She couldn't explain how her sister needed saving and then expect him to turn into Superman and sweep her away to safety. Grace couldn't dictate who Sophia fell in love with, and she couldn't prevent her from throwing her life away on a selfish jerk like Deezee.

Grace knew that. She did. She just wished…

She looked at the cypress tree again, a single, tall pillar of green in the middle of an acre of asphalt. A lonely pillar. "I wish I was as good as you are at imagining that everything will work out okay."

He turned toward her, laying his arm along the back of the bench. She was aware that his hand rested on the bench just behind her shoulder blades, right behind her spine, the very spine she needed to stiffen.

"Is everything not okay with you?" he asked.

She didn't want to have a spine of steel. She wanted to melt into his arms. "Isn't everything not okay with everyone? We all have our little troubles, right? Everyone's fighting their own battle."

She was babbling, fighting the desire to lean into him, into Alex Gregory, MD, according to the embroidery on his coat. *Can I call you Alex? Tell you all my worries?*

"Grace, you can talk to me."

Okay, that was a little scary. He was like the perfect guy.

But he was a doctor. He meant she could talk to him about medical things. "I don't think I've caught anything from her. I'm a generally healthy person."

He was studying her again. She didn't know when anyone else had ever looked at her so closely. She was only an assistant, for goodness' sake. Keeper of the lipstick and the schedule. What was there for him to see?

"I'm fine. Honest."

Alex Gregory, MD, began unbuttoning his white coat. He stood and shrugged out of it. The scrub pants she'd seen beneath his coat were matched by a loose green scrub shirt that had been pulled on over a long-sleeved white knit shirt.

"What are you doing?" she asked.

He sat back down, coat folded over his arm. "There. Now I'm not a doctor. Call me Alex. I'm not asking you about your health. You're not my patient. There are no legal obligations for me to report anything you want to tell me. Is there anyone you're scared of?"

"Listen, Dr. Gregory—"

"It's Alex."

His stethoscope was still hanging around his neck. She tried not to stare too long at the dusting of dark hair in the V-neck of his top. "You still look like a doctor."

He waited, silent.

"I'm sorry," Grace said. "It's not you. I just don't talk to anyone except Sophia. I can't. Everyone else, from the limo driver to a cashier at the grocery store, could make some money selling tales to tabloids, you know?"

"No, I don't know. I wouldn't know how to go about finding a tabloid to sell anything to."

"They'd find you."

"We're opposites, then. You can only talk to Sophia, and I can't talk about Sophia at all. Not legally. She's my patient, so the tabloids will be out of luck if they find me." He smiled at her a bit, a little crinkle at the corners of his eyes behind those frames. "I don't have any restrictions when it comes to you. Do you think the tabloids would offer me money to hear about you?"

"I'm nobody."

"Me, too. But I'd rather you called me Alex."

The little joke was pleasant, coming from such a serious man, but she couldn't find it in herself to return his smile. The desire to tell someone about her fears was painful. She looked over her shoulder out of habit. No one was in earshot, and Dr.—Alex—was sitting right here, all blue-eyed concern. God, she hadn't had a friend in a million years.

"Sophia's got herself mixed up with a terrible guy. A new boyfriend."

"Is that Deezee?"

"You've heard of him." She sat back, determined not to say anything else.

He tapped her back lightly with the hand that had been resting behind her shoulders. "I hadn't heard of him until ten minutes ago. You turned white when his name was mentioned."

"DJ Deezee Kalm? That doesn't ring any bells?"

He shook his head.

"He's the first guy she's been interested in for years, but I don't know why. He's awful for her. He's awful to her."

"This boyfriend is abusive?"

"Persuasive."

"Persuading her to do what, exactly?"

Grace wasn't sure how to answer that. Everything sounded melodramatic. Deezee was persuading her sister to throw away her career. Persuading her to destroy her own reputation. Persuading her to push away her own baby sister.

"Nothing that's really illegal." Even yelling at a police officer wasn't illegal. It was just horrible.

The thought of police made her think of the other patient Alex was dealing with this afternoon. "Oh—did you think he was like a Mr. Burns? Nothing like that. Deezee has just been persuading her to be mean to me. Not exactly a crime, is it?"

But how nice that Alex had been worried about her, like a big brother. She felt tears threatening. She started to get up, ready to go back inside.

He stopped her with a question. "How long has this been going on?"

She was startled into silence. He wanted to know more, even though she'd given him the easy out. Without physical abuse, it was hard to explain how poisonous Deezee was. A boyfriend was setting one sister against the other—no big deal, not enough to make an episode of reality television. Alex could easily dismiss her complaint as drama, but the way he'd said *How long has this been going on?* sounded like he thought *this* was significant. She could have kissed him for taking her seriously.

"They met at a thing in Telluride, three months ago. He's not as big a star as Sophia is, not nearly, but he hired a very well-known publicist. That's who introduced them.

Sophia never would have met him, otherwise. She doesn't do the club scene, or at least she didn't do the club scene before Deezee. She doesn't know any of the D-list wannabes that he hangs out with, and—" She clapped her hand over her mouth, mortified. "That sounded so snobby."

Her parents had raised her better. Each kid at school was to be treated the same, whether one wore expensive sneakers or one didn't. Having money hadn't made kids superior then, and being more famous didn't make her sister superior now.

Except it did. Those things mattered in Hollywood.

"She *is* an A-list celebrity. She earned that. It's not a matter of being photogenic or even being a good actress. She never fails to make her call. She's always prepared. I know I sounded bad just now about the D-list, but Sophia isn't snobby like that. By the time she leaves a set, the entire crew is always in love with her because she's nice to everyone. It's kind of sad that saying hello to the other people on the set is enough to make you stand out, but that's Hollywood, I guess. Anyway, her good reputation makes people want her on their projects."

She knew she was babbling, but the floodgates were open. "It's also Hollywood to lose your A-list status in the blink of an eye. Right now, Deezee has her dancing to his tune. The best scripts in circulation are sent her to read, but she's blowing them off in order to party with him. Deezee says he needs her, and she goes running."

"It sounds like the D-list guy is hoping her A-list status will elevate him."

"Exactly. Yes, exactly." Grace realized she'd reached out and clutched his forearm for emphasis. Despite the lightly chilly Texas air, she could feel the heat of his skin through the white shirt. His arm was solid in her grip. She meant to let go, but instead she gave his arm a little shake in her frustration. "How can you see it so easily, and she can't see it at all? I've pointed it out to her, but it's like talking to a child who doesn't want to believe that eating a bucket of candy is the reason she's sick to her stomach. I'm the one that's getting sick of it. We spent ten years building up to where we are now, and she's managing to destroy it in three months."

Grace did let go of his arm then. "Everything is going downhill. She's starting to act like him, disrespectful in public. Worse, she's being disrespectful *to* the public. Invitations have dried up, because no one wants her to bring Deezee to their event. The job offers will dry up next. The money will dry up. He's hurt her reputation, her finances— heck, he's even given her pneumonia."

Alex raised a brow at that. "He had an upper respiratory tract infection?"

She shooed away an imaginary bug. "I'm on a roll. I'm blaming him for everything, okay?"

Alex made a little sound of amusement, and Grace found herself doing something she never thought she'd do: laughing at the situation. Chuckling, at least. For a moment, anyway.

Her smile faded. "It's embarrassing, the way she talks to me now. I'm not normally a pushover. You probably find that hard to believe."

"Not at all. You didn't let me push you around when I was being short with you. I'm sorry, again, for shutting you down when you first asked to speak to me alone."

"You didn't know what I wanted to speak to you about."

"You're letting me off the hook pretty easily. That makes you kind as well as brave." He moved his arm, a simple shifting along the back of the bench, but his fingertips grazed her shoulder as he did. Did he linger? Had he touched her on purpose?

Please. She wanted to be touched. *More.*

She had no one to talk to but Sophia, no one to even hug except Sophia. Alex was too tempting. He was sympathetic and interested and warm, physically warm. And tall. With amazing blue eyes.

He almost touched her. She saw his gaze drop to her shoulder, but he stopped himself and raised his eyes to hers instead. "You were brave enough to report a crime today. I'm sure you are brave enough to find yourself a new job. You should work for someone who appreciates you."

It was either the conviction in his words or the kindness in his eyes that just about undid her. Whichever it was, her throat felt suddenly tight with emotion, making her voice sound husky. "She's my sister. I have to keep trying. I can't just let her crash without trying to get her to put on the brakes, you know?"

He hesitated only a moment. He set his hand on her shoulder, and gave her a firm squeeze, solid and warm, a masculine touch.

"Family."

That was all he said. One word. It was the bottom line, she realized. It was her purpose in life, to take care of her family. Her only family.

It felt like finding an oasis in a desert. Someone understood.

But then Alex let go. He looked resigned even as he gave her a small smile. "I hear sirens coming. My break is going to be over whether I want it to be or not." He stood, so she stood with him. "Are you going to be able to handle Deezee when he arrives?"

"He won't arrive. He can't. Sophia's contagious. You said so."

"Yes, but only for about forty-eight hours. She shouldn't

fly for a week, but she won't be contagious for long. Antibiotics are effective."

Her heart sank. "I thought I had a week, maybe a month. I need to keep her in Texas as long as possible. We've only been here a day, and already I've caught some glimpses of the real Sophia returning."

In silence, he began putting his coat back on.

"Couldn't you tell her she'll be contagious for a month?"

He pushed his glasses into place with his knuckle. "She's my patient. I won't lie to her."

Lying to celebrities was a given in Hollywood. *You don't have to wear anything you object to. There will be plenty of time to rehearse. This interview will only take five minutes, then we'll get you some lunch.* Telling Sophia she was contagious for a teensy bit longer than she really was barely counted as a fib in Hollywood. At least Grace's lie was for Sophia's own good.

"Um…could you not tell her how long she'll be contagious?"

He looked at her in silence, and she imagined all kinds of disapproval focused on her through those lenses. Clark Kent never told a lie, if Grace remembered her superheroes correctly. Her sister would like dating a man who didn't lie to her.

"I'm not asking you to lie, just not to mention it if she doesn't ask." The sirens were getting closer by the second, feeding some sense of urgency that Grace hadn't known was building. "The contagious thing is all I can think of to keep Deezee away from us."

Alex put his hands in his pockets. His poker face was back in place, but after a small eternity, he sighed. "I'm sure the nurse has given her the discharge orders by now. Unless she requests to see me specifically, she and I are done talking. Whether or not you choose to lie to your sister is something I can't control."

They were done. Alex was going to leave her. She'd be on her own with Sophia again, with no one else to talk to, no one who shared her concern. "When can we see you again? I mean, when does she follow up with you?"

"Unless she takes a sudden turn for the worse or spikes a significant fever, she should finish her antibiotics, travel home when she feels well enough and see her regular physician for follow-up."

This was goodbye, then.

No, no, no. She needed to think of something, but with the sirens closing in and the clock running out, she could only fall back on what she knew. Sophia was a powerful draw for most men, and Grace had the valuable commodity of access. "I'm sure Sophia would like to thank you properly when she's feeling better. If you give me your number, I can call you and we could set up a time for coffee or something."

"That isn't entirely appropriate. I don't normally visit a patient in their home—or hotel room. It stretches the limits of the doctor-patient relationship."

Desperation made her bold. "Let me give you my number, in case you change your mind."

She didn't have her tote bag with her. She found one of Sophia's gum wrappers in her pocket, but she had nothing to write with. Alex had a couple of pens clipped onto the edge of his pocket. He made no move to hand her one.

The ambulance pulled under the portico with a deafening noise. Grace winced, but she only had seconds. She grabbed a pen, scribbled her number on the paper side of the foil wrapper, and shoved the pen and the little silver square into his pocket.

He only raised one brow at her.

"I'm not your patient," she shouted over the sirens, "so you can call me."

The sirens cut off. Doors started slamming and personnel ran to open the back of the ambulance. Still facing her, Alex took one step backward, then two. "Stay safe. Don't climb on any rubble like your sister, and don't take any garbage from Deezee. Goodbye, Grace."

Then he turned around and joined the paramedics as they all jogged back into the building, pushing a gurney between them, calling out numbers to one another. Alex gave orders in Latin. He was saving someone else.

Grace stayed, rooted in one spot, stuck in Sophia's world.

Come back, Alex. Save me.

Chapter Seven

Grace had never been kicked out of a hotel before.

The South by Southwest festival had the entire city booked, and someone else had already paid for the suite she was trying so desperately to keep.

The hotel's general manager had given up any pretense of a friendly Texas drawl about twenty minutes ago. His words were brisk and his manner was as cold as the marble floor of the foyer. "The Presidential Suite was reserved a year in advance. We must honor that reservation. The bellhops will help you with your luggage, and the valets will call you a cab downstairs."

"Yes, but to where should we take the cab?"

He pressed his lips together. Grace knew he wanted to tell her to go to hell.

"You cannot stick Sophia Jackson in a cab and have her drive in circles around Austin, for goodness' sake." She smiled as she said it. *Wouldn't that just be so silly, Mr. Manager?*

"We did our best to find you another hotel room. I regret that South by Southwest has the city completely booked. Otherwise, we would have certainly extended Miss Jackson's stay." He raised his voice as he looked past Grace toward the suite's living room, where Sophia was doing a fine job of following Dr. Gregory's orders, reclining on the sofa while keeping her sprained ankle propped up on the armrest. "The cab could return you to the airport, perhaps. Your reservation was only for one night. We agreed to a late checkout, but it is nearly seven o'clock in the evening. You must leave."

Grace gritted her teeth. "Miss Jackson was in the hospital this afternoon. The doctor said she cannot fly today. I have a letter for the airlines explaining the medical necessity of changing her flight. That means it is a necessity for us to stay here, as well."

"Perhaps the hospital would care to provide you with a room, since they provided you with the letter."

Two bellhops stood like good soldiers, flanking the door. They had to be the two biggest bellhops on staff, hearty Texas boys who'd probably grown up eating steak on a cattle ranch. Despite their organ-grinder-monkey costumes, they were here to serve as bouncers, not bellhops. Sophia Jackson and her entourage, which consisted of one personal assistant, were being kicked out of this hotel. Deezee and his crew hadn't even had a chance to show up and trash it first.

Somehow, Grace kept her spine stiff with a dignity she didn't feel. "If you'll just give me a few more minutes, the director of Texas Rescue and Relief is going to call me momentarily. She's trying to find Sophia another place to stay."

"If there were another room available in the city, we would have secured it for you. The Hotel Houston prides itself on the highest level of guest care."

Oh, obviously. Grace nearly choked on the sarcastic reply. Antagonizing the general manager of the hotel wouldn't help her right now.

Sophia began another coughing fit.

Grace grasped at her only straw. She raised her voice for the benefit of the bellhop bouncers as she spoke to the manager. "The doctor said she's highly contagious right now, but since her ankle is also broken," a slight exaggeration, hardly a fib, "one of your bellhops will need to carry her to the elevator. I hope your staff is up to date on their flu vaccines."

The bellhops looked at one another in gratifying concern as Sophia sounded like she was hacking up a lung.

"We have a wheelchair for emergencies." The general manager nodded at one of the bellhops, who left the suite immediately, no doubt as eager to get away from Sophia's germs as he was to locate a wheelchair.

Grace hoped it would take a long time to find it. She looked at the cell phone in her hand, but the screen was still dark. The director of Texas Rescue had rather coolly informed her that she would ask if any Texas Rescue personnel were willing to put up two adults for a week in their own house. Knowing one of those two adults was sick with pneumonia made it unlikely, as she was sure Grace understood, but if she was successful, she'd call Grace.

She hadn't called.

No one in Texas Rescue seemed very enchanted with Sophia Jackson after her grudging appearance at the ribbon cutting. Grace had seen the videos on social media during the cab ride back to the hotel. Her sister had clearly caused her own injury, stomping into an area marked with bright orange off-limits signs. Six-second Vines and little gifs with grammatically incorrect captions were now posted all over social media. Bloggers and meme makers had helpfully circled all the warning signs in bright colors. *When Princessezz No Read*.

Sophia Jackson, who three months ago was a smart actress who made smart movies, had become a joke.

Threatening to sue Texas Rescue hadn't been the way to make them open their guest bedrooms, either. Grace didn't know what to try next if no one in the organization took pity on them. She looked over her shoulder at Sophia. Yesterday's complimentary fruit platter, a gift from the hotel before the Jacksons had refused to leave on time, adorned the coffee table like a work of art. It was an easy reach from the couch. Sophia ate a strawberry.

Grace's stomach rumbled. Her phone stayed dark. The manager stared her down.

A knock at the door made everyone jump. The bellhop practically ran to the door, as if Grace might try to beat him to it. A police officer in a blue uniform, badge and gun on display, strode into the hotel room. His radio loudly sounded off with some official dispatcher talk.

"Seriously?" Sophia said, lifting her head and pitching her half-eaten strawberry onto the coffee table. "You called the goddamned cops on us?"

The manager was looking smug, but the cop was looking from the bellhop to the manager to Sophia, and the look on his face was definitely confused. Grace had barely had a second to wonder what the policeman had expected to see when Dr. Gregory walked in.

She would have been as surprised to see the president of the United States walk into the presidential suite. Alex was still wearing his green scrubs, but the stethoscope was missing and he'd pushed up the long sleeves of that white undershirt. His day's razor stubble was reaching beard status. He looked tired, but he was looking for her, because he stopped and nodded at her once he saw her.

Sophia commanded center stage from her sofa. "You know what they say about men who have to compensate by calling in cops." She'd propped herself up on her elbows, taking in the scene. When all the men looked at her, she arched back a little bit and gave her blond hair a shake. The look she leveled on the manager conveyed both confidence in herself and derision toward him. "Were you afraid of me? Thought you needed a *bigger* man to back you up?"

The way she pronounced *up*, popping the *p* sound through her strawberry-stained lips, made Grace want to blush. She didn't dare make eye contact with Alex.

The manager snapped his fingers at the bellhop. "Charles, please go into the bedroom and get Miss Jackson's luggage for her."

"Don't you dare touch my stuff," Sophia said.

The bellhop froze in place, looking like he'd rather be anywhere else.

Grace smiled in vain. "You can't get our luggage, you see, because it isn't packed yet. It's just a big empty suitcase."

"I suggest you pack quickly," the manager said. "The police don't have all day. You can wait for your phone call in the lobby."

"We cannot wait in the lobby." Grace spoke through a clenched jaw, but she couldn't keep smiling and being deferential forever. "She's Sophia Jackson."

"I'm well aware of that."

"She was in *Space Maze*. That's a huge sci-fi hit, and the reason you're out of rooms is because South by Southwest is in full swing. Your hotel is full of *Space Maze* fans." It was another small lie. The indie music and film festival wasn't the same thing as a sci-fi movie convention, but accuracy didn't matter right now. "They'll mob her. Then you really will need the police, because she'll be in danger on your property." And that much was too true.

Alex stepped into the center of the room. The manager, bellhops, cop and movie star were arrayed all around him. He rested his hands on his hips and looked right at Grace. "I seem to have walked into the middle of something here."

She took a breath to explain, ready to plead her case one more time, but Alex slowly winked at her.

He didn't break his poker face, but that wink...

He'd walked into the middle...

Was he- was he making a *pun* while she was being kicked out into the street?

"And you are?" the manager intoned in what was now some kind of British butler's voice.

"Dr. Alexander Gregory. And you are?"

Grace bit her lip. Alex did a better man-in-charge voice than the manager, probably because he was used to being in charge in the emergency room, where things were a lot more important than who got two queens and a sleeper sofa.

The manager was only halfway through giving his official title when the police officer interrupted him "I need to speak to Miss Jackson. It's time sensitive."

"Indeed. They were supposed to vacate the room by four o'clock—"

"He means there's a judge and a possible warrant waiting to be issued. We need to speak to Miss Jackson." Alex sounded calm, but there was something in his voice, a little impatience, perhaps.

"Ohmigod. What did I do?" Sophia definitely sounded less than calm. "I didn't do anything."

Alex actually rolled his eyes before turning toward the couch. "Everything's not always about you, Sophia. We need to talk to Grace."

Sophia didn't have a chance to recover from her momentary shock at being dismissed by Alex, because the bellhop arrived with the wheelchair. Alex and the police officer exchanged a look.

The officer held out his arms and made a general shooing motion toward the door with the clipboard in his hand. "Everybody out. I'm conducting an interview."

The manager thought about objecting, Grace could tell, but the officer didn't look like he was open to discussion. The manager followed his bellhops out the door.

The officer hesitated before shutting the door, looking from Sophia's cast boot to the wheelchair, but Alex shook his head. "That's her sister."

"Ah." The officer was subtle about it, but now he looked between bombshell Sophia and gray-clad Grace.

Yeah, I know. Never would have guessed, would you?

"If you'd rather speak in private, your sister could move into the bedroom," he said.

Sophia rolled her booted foot from side to side. "Only if you carry me, big guy. My little tootsies can't touch the floor."

Grace tried to ignore her sister and focus on Alex. "I thought you didn't want to visit a patient in her hotel room."

A ghost of a smile briefly touched his lips. "I discharged her this afternoon. Technically, she's no longer my patient, but I didn't come to see her, anyway."

"I thought maybe Texas Rescue had sent you over, but the policeman gave it away. You must have an update for me on Mrs. Burns, after all." Oh, but wouldn't it have been nice if Alex had been the person from Texas Rescue to offer her shelter from the angry hotel staff? It was a selfish wish. The officer's uniform, with its holster and handcuffs, was a vivid reminder that no matter how frustrating her situation was, another woman in Austin was in far worse straits. "Isn't that why you're here?"

The officer spoke. "I'd like to ask you a few questions.

You aren't obligated to answer, but I'm hoping you can help us."

"Yes, of course."

She followed the officer to sit at the dining room table. Alex sat in the chair next to hers, resting his forearms on the table. With his sleeves pushed up, she could see his arms were tan. A real tan, not a Hollywood spray tan. She already knew his skin was warm...

He caught her staring.

She was hungry, she was about to be homeless, but she forced herself to focus. He hadn't answered her question. "Why are *you* here with the police officer?"

"Because I knew you would say 'yes, of course' without stopping to think of yourself." He phrased it like a criticism, but the warmth in his ice-blue eyes made her feel like she'd been complimented. "I made you a promise back in the ER that I'd personally make sure any interview with the police was private."

"I wouldn't have interviewed her on a street corner with a megaphone," the officer said with some amusement in his voice.

Alex ignored him. "I also told you not to worry, that I'd handle the situation. If I gave your location to the police and went home while you got a surprise visit from law enforcement, I wouldn't be a man of my word."

A man of his word. She hoped Sophia had heard that. Her sister was the one who needed a kinder, better man. But honestly, if Sophia couldn't appreciate a man like Alex, then Grace was tempted to...well...tempt the man herself. If she could remember how.

What kind of sister am I? Alex is just what Sophia needs.

The police officer silenced his radio. "Shall we begin?"

Chapter Eight

So this is what an exhausted angel looks like.

Alex was tired, but he was accustomed to functioning while he was tired. It was part of being a doctor, something he'd been doing since his first year of medical school. Even earlier—he'd studied until dawn to pass organic chemistry and the other undergrad courses required to be accepted to med school.

Grace hadn't had his training. She looked more than sleep deprived; she was under significant stress. She looked fragile. Alex was glad he'd come.

The officer on duty was Kent Grayson, a longtime acquaintance through Texas Rescue. He'd come into the ER just as Alex was leaving, looking for a woman who'd encountered Mr. Burns earlier in the day, according to the wife's account. Alex had known with a sinking feeling that the woman must be Grace Jackson. He'd flipped the gum wrapper with her phone number through his fingers for a few seconds, then decided to hell with it: if Kent was going to the Hotel Houston to see Grace, so was he. He'd put the wrapper back in his pocket and grabbed the key to his truck.

"If Mrs. Burns is safe at the women's shelter now, then where do I fit in?" Grace asked Kent, but the possibility obviously hit her before she finished her own question. "The children. Did he hurt the children?"

"We don't want to give him the chance. He's being processed at the jail now, so Mrs. Burns and her advocate went to pick up the children to take them to the women's shelter. Unfortunately, the children are with a relative of the husband's, and she's refusing to let Child Services take them."

"The police can't take them?"

"If someone's in immediate danger, I don't need permission to go in and save them, but otherwise, I need a warrant. Since the husband's sister isn't actually harming the kids, we need a warrant to enter the home."

"So that's why there's a judge waiting. You need me to explain that I overheard him say he'd kill the kids? Let me get a pen."

She jumped up to help, but Alex stopped her with a hand on her upper arm, her soft sweater sliding over toned muscle beneath. "You didn't tell me that you and Mr. Burns spoke face-to-face."

"He just opened the curtains and said, 'Who are you?' and then I said we needed privacy and shut them. It was nothing, really. It took maybe two seconds."

"He saw you, and if you volunteer to give this statement, your name will be in court documents."

"I see where you're going with this." She sank back down to her chair. "That could be bad for Sophia's career."

"Grace, look at me. It could be bad for *you*, not Sophia. This man has a violent arrest history. He could decide to come after you for testifying against him. I wanted to be sure you know this is optional. You don't have to put yourself in harm's way."

"Her name will be redacted from her statement, actually." Kent took a blank form off his clipboard and slid it across the table to Grace.

Alex slapped his hand on it, stopping the motion. "Her name won't stay hidden if the case goes to trial and she faces him from the witness stand. Grace, it isn't mandatory for you to write a statement. We had a long discussion about this with the shelter's administrator before we came."

"Let me do my job here," Kent said.

"Grace can't make an informed decision if you don't give her all the information."

"I can't give her all the information if you do all the talking."

"Good one," Sophia called from her sofa. No longer lounging horizontally, she'd sat up and propped her booted ankle on the coffee table, next to what Alex assumed was an obscenely expensive fruit arrangement. "Point for the hot cop. This could be so much more entertaining, though. When a cop and a doctor walk into my hotel room in their Village People costumes, I expect them to start stripping."

A stupid grin broke Kent's serious cop expression, but Grace looked mortified.

Alex wanted to get this over with. Grace wasn't enjoying any of it. "Most states require medical personnel to report suspected child abuse, but Texas law requires all citizens to report what they know."

"I did report it," Grace said. "To you."

Kent stopped grinning and returned to cop mode. "Specifically, Texas law requires a report to either law enforcement or Child Protective Services. Doctors, school teachers and the like aren't considered the proper authorities."

Alex was impatient. "The shelter staff believes that you haven't broken any law. You aren't legally required to report anything in this case."

Grace was sitting with her hands on the table, her fingers interlocked, her knuckles white.

Kent took over. "The consensus is that there was no way for you to determine if you overheard a credible threat. You don't know the couple involved, you don't even know if they have children and so on. 'I'll kill you if you do this or that' is a pretty common threat that people make in the heat of the moment, and it usually means nothing. There's practically no chance that you'd be charged with failure to report child abuse. You still should be made aware of the law, though, and be given the opportunity. You never know if a judge might interpret the law differently in any particular instance."

To Alex's surprise, Sophia spoke up from her sofa. "Passive aggressive much? You tell her she doesn't have to write a report, then you threaten her that if she doesn't write the report, there's a chance a judge could interpret the law differently than your posse does. Then you tell her it's totally up to her to decide whether or not to take that risk. Thanks for coming here to jerk my sister around."

So, the movie star had some family loyalty, after all. Alex was glad, for Grace's sake.

"I think you've done nothing wrong and everything right, Miss Jackson." Kent leaned to one side to glare across the room at Sophia. "*Grace* Jackson."

Grace smoothed over her sister's interruption. "So what do you need from me, Officer Grayson? I'm worried about those children. I never doubted they existed."

Alex felt that sloppy bit of tenderness for her again. She was brave, she was selfless, and her spirit fit that angelic appearance, but he'd wanted to be here to make sure she was down-to-earth. Good people got caught in bad situations even when they were only trying to help.

"Alex gave the judge all he needs to issue a warrant," Kent said. "When he told the hotel staff the judge was waiting, he exaggerated. We'll have those kids safe with their mother before Burns can ask for bail, but as a police officer, it's my job to talk to every possible witness, even if I'm ninety-nine percent certain a prosecutor won't need the testimony."

Alex watched Grace. "It's that one percent chance I wanted to make sure you're aware of."

She twisted her fingers one more time, then lifted her chin and looked him in the eye—not Kent, but him. "This afternoon you thought I was brave. Now you don't want me to make a statement?"

"If this was the only way to help those children, it would be worth the risk. Sometimes, doing the right thing is dangerous."

He was hit by an old memory—*his mother unlocking her office late at night, too afraid to turn on the lights. She'd been a structural engineer, wanting the town to know their factory was not safe. She was betting her life that glasnost had weakened the old Soviet regime enough so that the factory workers would strike once they knew the danger, but the remnants of the Communist Party had suppressed her report.* Doing the right thing can be risky, *she'd told him. She wanted to make copies of the report that would circulate from house to house, even if she was jailed. Her hand had trembled as she'd pressed the green button on the battered Xerox machine.*

Grace's clenched hands trembled.

Alex placed one hand over hers. "But those kids are going to get picked up even if you don't agree to be a witness. To put yourself at personal risk for no reason is a waste. I don't want you to have even a one percent chance you'll get hurt."

There it was. Something about Grace spoke to his soul. Whether he ought to care or not, whether he *wanted* to care or not, didn't matter. He didn't want to see Grace Jackson hurt.

Sophia's voice jarred him back to reality. "Is this Burns guy rich?"

Grace and Kent and Alex all looked at one another around the table. The question seemed irrelevant, but Kent answered her. "Their address isn't in a very affluent part of town."

"Ours is." She popped another strawberry in her mouth and kept talking around the fruit. "This loser isn't going to buy a plane ticket to come out to California, anyway, but if he did, he'd have to get past walls and gates and security guards. Hell, the paparazzi would make him the best photographed criminal you ever tried to ID. If you want to do this, Grace, then do it."

Surprise, surprise. In her own obnoxious way, Sophia was supportive of her sister. Alex grudgingly revised his opinion of her up one notch.

Grace began to write. Her penmanship was neat, her movements quick and certain despite the fine tremor in her hand. In the end, it took less time for her to write the statement than it had taken for them to decide she should write it.

Kent filled out the rest of the form. Name, address, phone number, all asked with a smile, all given the same way. Alex wished he hadn't been such an ass when she'd tried to give him her phone number. What had he been afraid of? Violating patient privacy rules?

I'm not your patient. You can call me.

It had been hard to force that out of his mind while he'd dealt with the ambulance arrival.

"Thank you again for your help." Kent was leaving, all smiles, his mission accomplished. Alex watched Grace smile, too, as she shook hands and wished Kent luck.

Hot cop, Sophia had called Kent.

Alex rubbed his jaw, the scratch of his beard not helping his mood. Kent nodded a goodbye to him, looking like some kind of poster boy for the All-American clean-cut look. Alex looked like...

Aw, hell.

He looked like hell, and he knew it.

The door closed after Kent. Grace turned to Alex and held out her hand to shake his, too. "Thanks again for coming."

Things felt stilted between them, as if they weren't on the same side. The whole reason he'd come tonight was to be sure she had someone on her side.

He didn't let go of her hand. "For what it's worth, I think you did the right thing."

"Thank you." Her polite smile relaxed into something more genuine; he felt rewarded. "You were playing devil's advocate for me."

They let go of one another.

"So, is this goodbye again," she said, "or am I going to see you in a couple of hours?"

"This is goodbye." But he didn't like that feeling, either.

"Better start packing, Gracie." Sophia tucked her hands behind her head and settled back, putting her good leg up on the coffee table, too. "That manager is going to be back the second he sees that cop leave."

A knock on the door was immediately followed by the sound of a card unlocking it. In walked the same bellhops that had been here when he'd first arrived.

"Told you," Sophia said. "Losers."

The hotel had no respect for privacy. Alex waited, ready to chew out the manager, but the manager didn't walk in next. Instead, three maids pushed in a cleaning cart. Ignoring both him and Grace, the bellhop spoke to Sophia. "I'm sorry, Miss Jackson, but we got a call that the next guest has landed at the Austin airport, so we're to get the room ready immediately, and, uh…if you could…you know…"

Two maids disappeared into the bedroom, as the third maid began pushing in the dining room chairs they'd used. The sound of the shower being turned on in the bathroom jerked Sophia out of her lazy pose.

"Grace! Our stuff is in there."

"Okay, okay." Grace pressed her hands to her temples. Her fingers still had that fine tremor. "Let me think. I'll think of something. I just—maybe—maybe we could head out of town and start trying different exits. Once we are out of Austin, one of those interstate hotels is bound to have a room, right?"

"Go get our stuff."

"Right. I need to call the front desk."

"Go to the bedroom. Our stuff isn't at the front desk, Grace. Jeez."

But Grace was almost talking to herself now, moving to the old-fashioned house phone beside the couch. "We can't use an app to get a lift if we can't type an address in first. No cab is going to want to go on a wild-goose chase out of town. We'll rent a car. I'll drive a car. It's been months, but— Hello?"

He swore he could hear a tremor in her voice as delicate as the one in her hands, but then a maid fired up a vacuum sweeper.

Grace turned to him suddenly, phone pressed to one ear,

and raised her voice over the vacuum. "The main highway is I-35, right? I can't remember."

It hit him that more than stress could make a person's hand tremble. For a doctor, he'd been slow to notice the signs. Shakiness, confusion—she was on the verge of a breakdown, tears welling up in her eyes.

"Grace, when's the last time you had something to eat?"

She held up a trembling finger, asking for one minute while she listened to someone on the other end of the line, then covered her ear with her hand. The maids were all making clatter of one type or another. A second later, she turned away from him, and he knew from the movement of her hand that she was dashing a tear from one eye.

"Yes, I know, I know. I'm calling to ask if you could arrange a car? Not a limo. I need a car that I could drive myself."

"Grace." He walked closer and took the phone away from her ear. She let it go without a fight. "When is the last time you had something to eat?"

"I'm sorry. Did you need me to order some dinner?"

He hung up the phone.

Despite her sudden frown, tears started to fall. *Emotional lability, secondary to hypoglycemia.* He should have seen it sooner.

"It's going to be okay." Damn it, but he couldn't cross his arms over his chest or stick his hands in his pockets one more time. She swayed into him, and he put an arm around her. She felt soft and warm and real, but a hug was not what she needed right now. He turned her toward the empty couch that ran parallel to her sister's. "Sit."

He held out his hand toward Sophia, who'd just helped herself to some kind of apple carved into a flower. "Toss it here."

She was surprised enough that she obeyed him.

"Eat this, Grace. I promise, we'll have you feeling better in a few minutes if you do as I say. I don't suppose there's a minibar in here?"

Sophia jerked her chin toward a corner of the living room. "To hell with mini, they gave us a whole liquor store. I'm presidential, baby."

Alex pushed aside the bottles of top-shelf liquor in the brass and lacquered bar area. He didn't want the alcohol; he needed the mixers. He found a small bartender's can of orange juice, shook it, then poured it into a crystal highball glass. The maid chewed him out in a foreign language—not Russian—and stopped vacuuming in order to pluck the empty can off the shelving and wipe away an imaginary ring.

Fine. She had her job to do, he had his.

His new patient was as uncooperative as the maid thought he was being. Grace stood and managed two stumbling steps toward the bedroom before Alex got in front of her and physically blocked her way.

"It sounds like they're breaking all of our stuff," she said.

"You're not going anywhere until you take care of yourself first."

She tripped on her next step, but he steadied her with one hand and managed not to slosh the orange juice out of the glass at the same time. "Drink this."

She placed two palms on his chest for balance. Her fingers curled into his scrub shirt. Tears were welling in those brown eyes again. Knowing they were nothing more than a physical result of exhaustion and low blood sugar did nothing to lessen the tug he felt in response.

"I'm sorry," she whispered.

"There's nothing to be sorry for." His voice sounded gruff, and he knew it. He wasn't angry at her. He just resented that tug of sympathy. He hated having no control over his reactions to her. She made him feel... God, she made him *feel*.

She kept one hand on his chest for balance as she took the glass and downed the orange juice. It wasn't her fault he found her so damned appealing. He shouldn't have such a hard time treating an angel with some basic friendliness.

"All right, let's go pack your stuff together." He forced himself to smile at a perfectly lovely woman whose blood sugar had crashed. This was simple attraction, nothing more, nothing less. He could deal with it. "I'm going to keep an eye on you until you feel better."

Her answering slow smile reminded him less of a noble angel and more of a woman who'd had one drink too many. "Promise?"

"Sure."

"Good, because you're a man of your word."

He had a feeling the light-headedness from hypoglycemia mimicked the light-headedness she'd get from being intoxicated. The impression was helped by the highball glass in her hand.

She poked him in the chest with it now. "You're a really nice guy, even though you are hard to read. You have such a good poker face."

"And you have none," he murmured.

"I don't? Can you tell what I'm thinking?" She leaned in one inch closer to whisper to him. "I'm thinking that I'm glad I met you today."

"Thank you." He looked over her head to Sophia. "Does she always get like this when her blood sugar is low?"

"Nope. Usually, she gets all weepy."

He hadn't meant it as a trick question, but Sophia's answer made him angry. "Usually? So you knew that she was prone to low blood sugar, and you didn't remind her to eat something today?"

"I've been just a little bit sick myself, you know. Emergency room. Pneumonia. Any of that ring a bell?" But her uncaring, tough-girl defense didn't quite ring true. The way she looked at her sister confirmed it. Sophia the Diva felt some guilt. "She'll be fine in, like, ten minutes. You should give her another glass of juice."

He was a doctor. He knew how hypoglycemia worked, but instead of aiming a sarcastic comment at Sophia, he pushed Grace onto the couch to sit right next to her. He got another can of orange juice and tossed it at Sophia. "Pour it for her. Don't let her get up again. I'll go pack your suitcases."

She caught the can. "You'd better arrange that rental car first. I really can't sit in the lobby, hoping someone will find us a place to stay. It'll turn into a big mess. Grace wasn't exaggerating."

He kept walking toward the bedroom. "I'm not sticking her behind the wheel of a rental car ten minutes after a hypoglycemic episode."

"She'll be fine." He heard the pop of the can being opened, the pouring of the liquid into the crystal glass. "She'll perk right up in a second."

"I already feel better," Grace said, sounding anxious.

He stopped then and turned to assess her appearance.

"I'm so sorry, Sophie, I'll fix everything. I should've eaten something, but I just got busy. My bad."

"No." His voice sounded harsh.

Both women looked at him.

No, you will not keep trying to make Sophia happy. You won't apologize for things that aren't your fault. You won't shoulder every single responsibility alone.

"Drink that juice. Forget the rental car and the roadside motel hunt. You can stay with me."

Damn it, he sounded angry again. He shouldn't be. He was doing the right thing, and he knew it. It was just that sometimes doing the right thing was risky.

He left the two women on the couch and walked into the bedroom, where two maids had beaten him to the packing. An unzipped suitcase lay on the foot of the bed. One maid tossed a stack of folded clothes into the suitcase.

He leaned against the doorjamb and brooded about his unexpected houseguests.

What, exactly, was the risk here? What was he so damned afraid of?

That he'd catch pneumonia from a movie star? Not likely. He had the constitution of an ox after years as a doctor.

That he'd have his routine disturbed, that he'd have to share his living room and relinquish control of the TV? He spent most of his nights reading, anyway.

That he'd have to listen to Sophia complain and Grace apologize for a couple of days?

Ah, that was getting closer.

Grace Jackson. That was the risk. He could feel himself getting involved, actually starting to care about a woman who would disappear within the week.

The maid he could see through the bathroom door let loose with a string of foreign words that were surely curses. The maid was apparently repulsed by the amount of cosmetic bottles and jars she was tossing into a plastic bag that bore the hotel's logo. Her cursing fit his mood, too.

Grace Jackson had been stirring up his emotions all day. He ought to be glad that she was destined to return into the world of California celebrities within a week. After all, everyone disappeared sooner or later, whether he cared about them or not. His ER patients tended to disappear the same day. His family had taken longer, but he'd literally watched his father disappear on a seashore, growing smaller and smaller as the boat he and his mother had crowded onto sailed farther and farther out to sea, until finally the shore itself had disappeared.

His mother had disappeared, shoved into a car with black-tinted windows, gotten out of the Russian jail, disappeared again. Even now, as a successful professor, she still left Texas for long stretches of time, always on the go to a developing nation to set up another school. He wouldn't be surprised if he got a call that she'd disappeared in a third-world nation, taken hostage or caught in a rebel war. Even his coworkers disappeared without warning, called up by Texas Rescue to work at the sites of natural disasters.

Aleksander Gregorivich hadn't been able to control his life, but Alexander Gregory could. He'd chosen one city he liked and settled there. He worked at one hospital. His role with Texas Rescue was to be the physician who stayed to man the home front, pulling extra shifts, covering for those who disappeared when the mobile hospital was needed. He was anchored firmly to one place. He knew better than to get involved with anyone who might leave.

He was involved with Grace Jackson, though.

She would leave.

Still, helping her out was the right thing to do. For a week, he'd help a woman who was being overwhelmed, and he wouldn't be shocked when she left. There'd be no tearing of his soul, no broken heart like there'd been when his father had refused to board the boat or when his mother had been handcuffed by the secret police of a crumbling government.

The bathroom maid spotted him before she could sling the bag of cosmetics into the suitcase. He waited until she'd placed the plastic bag in the suitcase with exaggerated carefulness, then zipped up the suitcase. He hefted it off the bed, amazed at what was considered an overnight bag for a movie star and her assistant, and turned to leave.

Grace was standing there, soft sweater on her body, golden highlights in her hair. She'd recovered. He could tell by her alert expression and the faint blush of pink on her cheeks as she thanked him for the juice.

"And thank you for letting us stay at your place. I'm sorry to keep bothering you."

"You're no bother at all."

In this moment, Alex was glad that when she left the hotel, she'd be leaving with him.

He could regret taking the risk later.

Chapter Nine

Alex Gregory was a man who kept his word.

Squashed up against him in the cab of his pickup truck, Grace could also tell he was a man who kept in shape.

It seemed that half the vehicles on Austin's roads were pickup trucks. Luckily, Alex's truck had a bench seat that could hold three people. Since it had been hardest for Sophia to get in the cab with her injured ankle and clunky cast boot, she had, reasonably enough, demanded the seat closest to the passenger door. Grace had to sit in the middle, and since Sophia kept complaining about how uncomfortable she was, wiggling to sit at an angle to stretch out her leg, Grace was quite firmly pushed up against Alex.

He moved his arm to hit the turn signal and flexed his thigh to apply the brakes. Under those shapeless scrubs, she felt some totally masculine musculature in motion. Grace studiously kept her gaze on the traffic light out the windshield, trying to look like she wasn't aware of the hard body that was making her feel so very feminine in contrast.

"Move over," Sophia demanded.

Grace didn't mind that demand at all.

Alex didn't seem to mind much, either. He actually had a bit of a smile playing around his lips. Grace wasn't certain what had happened up in the presidential suite to change his opinion, but Alex seemed less disapproving of Sophia. Slightly less, but it was a start.

Grace knew she didn't have the power to make two people fall in love, but if she could get Sophia to see what it was like to spend a little time with a man who treated her well, maybe she'd snap out of this phase. After a week with Alex, maybe she'd be able to see Deezee in a new light.

If I don't steal Alex first.

She twisted her fingers together in her lap. When had she started having such awful thoughts? She'd never been jealous of Sophia in her life. Men wanted Sophia. They always had; they always would.

But Alex...

Grace had assumed he'd come to the hotel tonight as an excuse to see Sophia, but he'd spent all his time sitting next to *her*, Grace, and talking to her. In fact, the only discussion he'd had with Sophia had been about her, about when she'd last eaten and whether or not she should drive.

Her cheek brushed against his shoulder as he turned the truck away from the city lights. Yep, there was solid muscle under those scrubs.

Was it really stealing a man if he preferred her to begin with? There was something about the way he'd offered his truck and his home that implied they were for Grace. *I've got a spare bedroom for you. We'll find something for your sister to sleep on, too.* It was as if Sophia was the afterthought. Grace noticed it, because for her entire adult life, she'd only gone to places that tolerated her because she was part of Sophia's entourage. Tonight, she couldn't help but think that, despite the way Sophia was hogging more than half the bench seat, Sophia was only being included because she was tagging along with Grace.

Alex liked *her*. Grace. She was almost certain of it, although she hadn't done anything differently to catch his attention. She'd just been herself, and Dr. Alex Gregory had noticed her. To please Deezee, Sophia had changed her nightlife, her friends, her clothes, even her way of talking.

See, Sophia? You don't have to compromise to make a man love you. And you don't have to be with a man who hates your sister, either.

Sophia made a sarcastic comment about something on the side of the road, and Alex actually laughed.

Grace had hoped Sophia would dump Deezee if she was attracted to a normal guy here in Texas. But as Alex's body brushed hers as he pulled into his driveway, she reevaluated that. Wouldn't it be just as effective if Sophia saw Grace fall for a normal guy? If Grace let herself be treated right by, say, a handsome doctor from Texas Rescue, wouldn't Sophia see that Deezee didn't treat her as well as her sister's boyfriend treated her?

Talk about indulging in a fantasy scenario—but as Alex walked around the hood of the truck to get the door for Sophia, it actually seemed possible.

Sophia was hesitant to jump down from the high cab. Alex, being so wonderfully tall, was able to slide an arm behind Sophia's back, scoop another under her knees and simply lift her out of the truck.

He set her gently on the ground. "You should be able to walk in that boot. Try it and see."

At the hotel, Sophia had hopped on one bare foot to the wheelchair, and then Grace had put her spike-heeled sandal on her good foot for her, to keep her as elegant-looking as possible for the fans with cell phones who would see them leave the hotel.

Now, Sophia stood up straight on her high-heel-wearing good leg, which meant the flat boot didn't even touch the ground. Everyone laughed. Grace scooted to the edge of the bench seat, ready to hop down herself, but Sophia didn't move. Instead, Alex took a knee in front of Sophia. She leaned against the door jamb as she gingerly put her weight on her boot.

Alex unbuckled her sandal for her. He was smiling, his shaggy hair falling over his forehead in an appealing way as he looked up at her sister. "I don't know how women wear these things even when they aren't injured."

Sophia's hand rested on his shoulder for balance as she lifted her foot. In her coat dress, she could be a modern-day princess, bestowing knighthood on a man at her feet. Or he could be on bended knee, ready to give her a diamond ring.

Grace swallowed. They did look good together.

"Heels make our legs look great, don't you think?" Sophia asked Alex.

"I understand *why* women wear them." He slipped off her sandal. He stood again, bringing his face level with Grace's as she sat in the truck cab, but he was laughing down at her sister. "I'm just glad I don't have to wear anything like that."

Sophia actually smiled, not an actress's smile, and Grace watched the two of them talking, blue eyes matching bespectacled blue eyes.

They surveyed the walkway to the door. The porch lights shone off a sea of river rocks. Stepping stones were spaced to create a path. Grace craned her neck a bit to look past Sophia's head. Sophia would have to treat the stepping stones like lily pads, hopping from one to another, if she couldn't put her foot down yet. The house was a 1930s Craftsman-style home, complete with concrete stairs leading up to its square-pillared entrance. It made a pretty intimidating obstacle course for someone on only one foot.

"Oh, boy..." Sophia wrinkled her nose and looked up at Alex once more. "Could you have just provided burning coals for me to cross?"

"It looks impossible, doesn't it?" Alex picked her up again, carrying her like she was a bride. Sophia actually looked grateful. She wrapped her arms around his neck, her sandal dangling from one finger.

Grace half slid off the bench seat, falling the last few inches to the ground to land squarely on her own feet. She didn't need a man to lift her or carry her or ease her pain.

Sophia did. Grace should let Sophia have what she needed. Sophia had raised her after their parents had died. She'd tried to cook their mother's recipes. She'd made Grace do her homework. She'd dropped out of college for her, and she'd kept her by her side ever since.

Grace would walk over hot coals for her sister. The least she could do, now that Sophia was noticing Alex, was to stop selfishly wishing she could keep Alex for herself.

She'd fix this. She wouldn't allow herself to fall for Alex—or, at least, not fall any farther than she already had.

The little stab to her chest was her own fault. She shouldn't have started the truck ride by letting herself fantasize about the man her sister needed.

I'm sorry, Sophia. I'll be good from now on.

Personal assistant. Sister. Grace couldn't even imagine herself as a competitor, not with the charismatic Sophia Jackson, not even for a man like Alex Gregory.

There was a beautiful woman in Alex's bed.
Too bad he was stretched out on his couch.

Technically, there were women in his beds, plural. His house had two bedrooms, and each bed held a sleeping woman, but thoughts about only one of those women kept him awake. Grace Jackson, whom he'd thought he'd never see again at five o'clock this evening, was now sleeping on his pillow. The knowledge kept his body taut and his adrenaline too elevated for sleep.

Otherwise, his couch would work fine as a bed. One reason he'd bought the modern black couch was because it was extra long, an excellent trait in a piece of furniture when one fell asleep on the first available horizontal surface after the odd twenty-four hour shift. But he didn't think it was good enough for Grace. He'd insisted she take his bed.

Grace had resisted, of course. There'd been no question that Sophia would help herself to the guest room. She'd taken off her cast boot and hit the mattress, completely unconcerned about her sister, leaving Grace and Alex to work out the rest.

I'll share the guest room bed with her. It'll be like the old days.

The old days, like when we had the Plague? She's contagious. Take my bed.

He'd pulled out a change of sheets from his hall closet, and they'd made up his bed together, a strangely intimate chore he'd never done with any other woman. If he and Grace had come here for sex, they could have fallen into bed together. But since they weren't intimate and she was his houseguest, he'd pulled out a fresh set of sheets like a good host. And yet, plumping pillows, stretching sheets taut—it had felt like foreplay to him.

She probably thought he was a germaphobe. If she was generous, she might think he was a geeky doctor who cracked lame jokes about plagues and worried about upper respiratory tract infections in bed. Hell, he'd even reminded Sophia to wash her hands more often than usual until the antibiotics kicked in.

He shifted on the couch and scrubbed his hand over his face, feeling the heavy stubble again. He didn't look like a neat-freak germaphobe. He probably looked like a hippie who'd been lost in the wilderness for a week, scrounging in the woods for food.

In other words, Grace had no reason to lie awake on fresh sheets, obsessing about him.

He could not stop thinking about her.

In the light of day, he'd spent his time wondering why she was under sister's thumb. He understood a little better now that he'd seen some flashes of loyalty from Sophia. She'd backed up Grace when it came to the domestic violence case, a point that had softened his attitude toward Sophia just a bit.

But he knew the patterns and habits of domestic violence. He couldn't help but recognize the parallels in the way Sophia treated her own sister. Her own bad behavior was excusable —*I had pneumonia*— but Grace's failures were not—*You need to fix it, you need to move over, you need to find us a place to stay*—an unreasonable demand during South by Southwest. He'd dealt with enough domestic violence to see the one-sided relationship. Could Grace see it? Could he help Grace see it in the short time she'd be in his life?

Those were the thoughts that had consumed him while he and Grace were fully dressed and on their feet. Now, in the still of the night, his thoughts were considerably less philosophical. He was horizontal and half naked, wearing only plaid pajama pants. Grace was horizontal. Was she half-naked? Did she wear pajamas, comfortable and worn? Did she wear a nightgown, silky and new? Did she wear anything at all?

The possibility that Grace was sleeping nude between his sheets was the reason he was still awake. *Use your imagination*, he'd told Grace earlier, when they'd taken a break on the bench. He'd never expected to use his imagination tonight in quite this way, but it was easy to picture her. Grace was beautiful. Nothing like her sister, thank God. Sophia's sort of professional beauty was an achievement, a victory over nature. Grace's beauty was touchable, soft, genuine.

He'd had a great chance to check out her curves when she was pressed up against him in the truck. For once, he'd found Sophia's bossy routine amusing. Every time she'd barked *move over*, he'd wanted to say *thank you*.

He was paying for that pleasure now. The curve of Grace's shoulder, the way her hair felt as it swept over his own skin—he could imagine the angel in his bed all too vividly. His muscles were taut, demanding that he go to her. Muscle couldn't distinguish between the fantasy of what he'd like to do and the reality of what was acceptable. Sexually, he felt thick and full and aching for more.

He sat up, determined to get control so he could get some sleep. He headed for the kitchen and a midnight glass of milk.

The reality was, sharing a bed with Grace was off the table this week. She'd be heading back to California and a life that kept her tied to someone else, twenty-four hours a day. He yanked open the fridge door and blinked into the sudden light, deliberately obliterating the images he'd drawn in the dark. Cold air cooled the bare skin of his chest. Women who disappeared held no appeal for him.

Liar. She's got more appeal than you know what to do with.

He took the milk out of the fridge. In order to shut the

door, he took a half step back, and backed right into Grace herself. He hadn't heard her come in to the narrow galley kitchen. She looked warm and rumpled and delicious in the appliance light.

Pajamas. The answer to his earlier question was pajamas. They weren't worn and comfortable, but satin. The material flowed over her body, white satin conforming to the shape of her breasts like liquid. His reaction to the sight of her couldn't be denied. He slammed the fridge door shut, plunging them both into blinding darkness. Retinal chemistry bought him time to fight another type of chemistry.

"I couldn't sleep," she said, her voice as appealing at midnight in his kitchen as it was at noon in the ER. Her feet were bare, which was probably why he hadn't heard her.

"Want a glass of milk?" His voice sounded stilted, stiff.

"Does milk really make you sleepy? Scientifically speaking?"

A medical question. How could she ask it in such a bedroom voice?

It was hard to not touch her, even if she thought of him as more of a doctor than a man. In one hand, he clutched the milk carton. He set his free hand on his hip rather than hers.

"It's a myth, but if it makes you feel better, have a glass. You could use the calories after forgetting to eat all day."

"I made up for it with the pizza tonight. Thank you for ordering that."

"You already thanked me."

She lapsed into silence. Had he been rude? His eyes were rapidly adjusting to the dark. There was a sheen to her pajama top in the small light from the microwave's clock. The aroused peak of her breast was not a trick of the light.

He tore his attention away from her body. If her vision

was adjusting as fast as his, he didn't want to be caught staring at what he was craving.

"Sorry," she breathed quietly. "I'm in your way, aren't I?"

But she didn't move.

He realized she wasn't looking at his face at all. Her gaze was on his biceps, flexed as he held the milk carton. Her chest rose and fell with a quickening breath as her gaze moved across his body to his chest.

I can see you staring at me.

She moistened her lips, her eyes traveling lower, following a center line down his body, lingering in the area of his abs—his navel?—then lower.

You want me.

The knowledge changed the game. He knew what a woman wanted when her eyes went all heavy-lidded and her attention was all on his body. Grace's awareness redoubled his.

He wanted her, too. He'd wanted her all day.

She was going to leave, permanently. He even knew when she'd leave, but at this moment on this night, it didn't matter. Desire was obliterating his ability to think in the long term.

He watched her tentative fingertips reach for his body. The pad of her thumb brushed the bare skin of his waist as her fingertips trailed over the loose elastic of his flannel pants. He tossed the carton of milk onto the counter, startling her, so he used his now-empty hand to soothe her with a stroke down the soft length of her hair. He scooped a handful into his palm, all its golden highlights hiding in the dark. They were safe and alone at midnight, he and she.

"Grace." Her name sounded so much like a prayer, a husky benediction, a gift.

"I can't."

She stepped back, her hair sliding over his palm until it was gone. He let his hand drop to his side.

He wouldn't ask why not. He'd only met her today. Her sister had been brought in to the ER sometime after lunch; it was only midnight now. Less than twelve hours he'd known her, and in those twelve hours she'd been through stress of every kind.

All the more reason to hold her, his mind whispered. *Touch her, soothe her, make her worries disappear for a while.*

"I just can't," she whispered. She turned on her heel and disappeared.

That old feeling of abandonment was fleeting, because she hadn't truly disappeared. He knew where she was: in his bedroom, under his covers. Lying there, wanting him.

He almost gulped the ice-cold milk straight from the carton, but he had guests. He poured the milk into a glass and downed it in strong swallows, feeling the drink cool his mouth and throat. It didn't wash away the image of Grace on his pillow, in his room, *wanting him.*

He shook his head at his own intensity. They felt the same way about one another. If it was too soon tonight, there was still tomorrow. She wasn't leaving for a week. There were more midnights to be had. Time stretched before him, his ally.

He headed back to his couch to try again to sleep. The anticipation of spending tomorrow with Grace was a pleasure so sharp, it was nearly a pain in itself.

Wasn't that how life always worked? Pleasure followed by pain. Since childhood, he'd known that happy moments were followed by grief. A trip to the beach with Mama and Papa was followed by a raid on his home. Receiving a loaf of bread at a refugee camp was followed by a fistfight to defend it. He'd spent many years avoiding pain, which meant he'd spent many years avoiding pleasure.

But tomorrow...

He'd forgotten how intense the pleasure could be. The brush of a woman's fingertips and the softness of her long hair, the knowledge that she found him as desirable as he found her—those were things that could make joy explode in a man's chest.

He wanted to savor the joy.

He could deal with the carnage from the explosion later.

Chapter Ten

Alex woke to sun shining through his patio door. The plants on his back porch were soaking it up, just as he'd calculated they would when he'd designed his landscape. Sun in the morning, shade in the afternoon, cactus flowers that bloomed at night.

Last night...

He was only slightly stiff from sleeping on the couch. It wasn't the first time he'd fallen asleep here, but it was the best reason he'd had for spending the night in his living room. He hadn't succumbed to exhaustion after hours in the ER. Instead, he'd slept on the couch in order to give Grace Jackson his bed—but at midnight, she'd been in his kitchen, letting her fingertips graze over his skin.

Today was going to be a good day. Dappled sun reflected off the racing bikes he kept mounted on the wall when he wasn't riding them. The polished concrete floor of his living room shone like clean glass. All was right with the world. He had the day off work. He had a beautiful woman to get to know better. And then tonight…

He shouldn't get ahead of himself. It was only morning. Pancakes seemed like a good way to start a good day. Fortunately, he hadn't drunk all the milk last night—

A woman's sudden cry had him rolling to his feet on full alert.

"He can't! He couldn't!"

Princess Eva Picasso stumbled into his living room, blond and bare-footed, hopping and hissing in pain every other step, eyes glued to the phone in her hand.

Not a princess. This was no movie scene. Sophia was a real person, Grace's sister, and she had a look of absolute horror on her face. Alex instinctively took a step toward her, ready to help.

She looked up from her phone and seemed shocked to see him. "Where's Grace?"

"She slept in my room."

Abruptly, Sophia turned and headed down the hallway. Her first step made her yelp in pain, but she kept going around the corner. "Grace—oh, Grace. He's such a cheating bastard."

Alex heard his bedroom door open and slam shut.

He walked into the hallway and listened for a moment. He heard women's voices, one hysterical, one soothing. His idyllic day with Grace, he realized, had depended on Sophia staying in bed and sleeping through her pneumonia. Damn it. He'd been awake maybe sixty seconds, and his plans were already shot.

Sophia's presence jolted him back to reality. What had seemed possible in the dark looked unlikely now. Whatever the problem was, it hadn't been medical, but Sophia's dramatic reaction made it medical now. She'd undoubtedly bought herself another day or two in the cast boot by running through the house without wearing it.

Instead of whipping up pancake batter, he went into the kitchen and started putting ice in a plastic bag. Medical care was the only kind of help he had to offer. This emotional crisis was beyond his expertise.

He'd studied emotions from a medical standpoint, of course. Research had proven that unrelenting stress had health consequences. His childhood had been full of crises, which made it all the more important for him to keep his adulthood under control. The only stressor allowed in his life was his job.

That was enough. An emergency doctor's routine was never routine, although the chronic frustrations that were punctuated by high-adrenaline moments of trauma were predictable, in their way.

To balance his on-duty stress, he kept his off-duty life calm. His home was clean and uncluttered, his cycling events were planned and trained for months in advance, his diet was healthy. With a lifestyle built on that solid base, he didn't fear being derailed by an occasional indulgence: a beer with coworkers, a late night of billiards, pancakes with white flour and sugar.

A week with Grace Jackson.

He should be fine with a short-term fling, but as he sealed the plastic bag of ice, it didn't feel so simple. Which was he was afraid of—that the week wouldn't happen, or that it would?

Or that she could be the one indulgence that derails my life?

Impossible.

It'll happen when a goat eats a wolf, his mother's favorite phrase. He nodded to himself. A week with a woman, no matter how appealing she was, couldn't change his calm and orderly world.

Or could it? Yesterday, he'd spent his only break talking with her on a bench. After work, he'd gone to her hotel to sit in on a police interview. He'd brought her into his home. He was tolerating the presence of a diva with pneumonia for her sake.

It's been less than twenty-four hours since you laid eyes on her. What do you think a week will do to you?

He threw the bag of ice onto the concrete floor, shattering the cubes.

He was in control. The crushed ice would conform to the ankle, reducing inflammation more efficiently. He bent down to scoop up the plastic bag, shook it out, and placed it flat in the freezer, ready for his patient when she emerged from the bedroom.

With her sister, of course. Grace would emerge after soothing Sophia and fetching her cast boot, at a minimum. She'd lose any trace of the early-morning sleepy look before he had a chance to savor it.

Poor Grace.

She didn't need a fling with him. She needed a new career, if not a new sister. Any kind of decent man would focus not on sleeping with her, but on helping her. That was the important matter. That was why he'd offered to take her in. To help her.

Alex pulled out an iron skillet and set it on the stove. He might as well make the pancakes. It was still his day off work. It was painfully obvious that Grace never had a day off work, but she could eat the pancakes, anyway. They'd be something comforting to balance the chaos of her life.

It was a shame she'd never know they'd been meant for seduction.

Grace ate her pancakes on the back porch, alone.

She had her reasons. For one, the backyard was a landscaping work of art, incorporating rocks and cactus and shade trees that she was certain would exceed any Californian's eco-friendly, water-conserving, xeriscaping standard. She needed the soothing surroundings because of reason number two: Sophia was being nice to Alex.

This morning, Alex had been concerned about Sophia, icing her ankle and bringing her pancakes after pouring exactly as much syrup as she'd requested. Thank goodness Grace hadn't done anything too stupid last night. He must not have been thinking sensual thoughts about her in the dark after all. It was obvious this morning that he cared for Sophia.

Incredibly, the odds of Sophia falling for Alex were much higher today because of reason number three: Deezee had cheated on Sophia. Photos of Deezee with some girl he'd met at a bar were all over the internet this morning.

The Deezee phase was abruptly over. Her sister was furious, and rightfully so, but Grace felt like the weight of the world had been lifted from her shoulders. She was afraid she'd burst into a round of the "Hallelujah Chorus," or at least smile, so she'd taken her plate of pancakes and headed outside. What kind of sister would she be if she was caught smiling at those incriminating photos?

In several of them, Deezee had been talking to an unidentified woman in a club, which wouldn't have been so damning if his hips hadn't been pressing her up against a wall as they talked. One showed them holding hands as they waited at a valet stand. Somehow, the hand-holding one looked more intimate to Grace than the wall one. In a final blow, someone had snapped him disappearing into a hotel room with his arm around the same girl, who barely looked old enough to be legal despite her very adult dress.

The dress was revealing and cheap, a knit with crooked seams being worn a size too small, something which Sophia had actually noticed. *She's got no class, no style, no money. She's not even a celebrity. What was he thinking? She can't be any help to him at all.*

Grace had refrained from hazarding a few guesses about what Deezee had been thinking. It seemed pretty obvious what kind of help Deezee expected the girl to be.

Grace ran the pad of her thumb along the rim of her plate. As tempting as it was to throw stones at Deezee, she felt terribly exposed in her own glass house. Last night, she'd been thinking about the same thing. Deezee had been dating one woman, but touched another. Not so different from Grace, who'd chosen one man for Sophia, but wanted to touch him for herself.

Wanted to? She *had* touched Alex. Very briefly, but the sensation was burned into her fingertips. Grace had fallen asleep believing he wanted her, too. He'd touched her hair, hadn't he?

Her hair. In the morning sunshine, she felt like an idiot. When a man desired a woman, really burned for her with passion, the only time he touched her hair was in some kind of a historical film, set in an era when a woman's hair was the only part of her body not covered in an acre of cloth. Grace had read way too much into it. He'd just brushed his hand down her hair the same way one might soothe a dog or cat.

Thank goodness she'd chickened out and run away. No harm done. He'd been able to serve her pancakes today with a friendly smile.

She should have been able to take the plate from him the same way, with no embarrassment at all, but no. She'd babbled something about how Austin had such mild weather and then she'd run outside.

Talk about a temporary solution. She couldn't stay out here for a week. She couldn't even stay for half an hour. Her sister needed her.

She peeked over her shoulder into the house. Through the sliding glass door, she could see her sister sitting on the couch, her head bowed with grief. Alex hadn't stayed to eat with her, after all. Grace felt guilty for leaving her alone. She should be there, helping her pick up the pieces. At least she and her sister wouldn't constantly be at odds anymore, now that the Deezee phase was over. It was time to go back inside.

Sophia didn't look up as Grace shut the sliding glass door behind herself. Her posture was so abject, Grace's guilt doubled. "How are you doing, Sophie?"

Sophia shrugged.

Grace came closer and saw the phone in Sophia's hand. Irritation warred with guilt. Alex probably would have sat with her while they ate, if only Sophia had been polite enough to make conversation with a human.

"Ready for more pancakes?" Alex called from the kitchen.

Sophia ignored Alex totally. Not wanting to be rude, Grace pretended she had an appetite. "That would be great, thank you."

She carried her plate into the kitchen. Alex was eating as he leaned against the counter, plate in one hand, fork in the other, finishing off a short stack. He smiled at her. "Eat them while they're hot, right?"

Something was hot, all right. She'd changed into jeans and a beige blouse, but Alex was still wearing the loose-fitting plaid pants from last night, the same eyeglasses from the day before. He'd added a blue T-shirt that hugged his body. His hair and beard might be scruffy, but that body was tight.

She'd dreamed about that body. What a surprise for her senses last night had been, walking into the kitchen to find him bare-chested in the light of the refrigerator. She'd already guessed in the truck that there was more muscle under those scrubs than met the eye, but she hadn't been prepared for quite *that* athletic of a physique. Clearly, when a doctor's white coat had to be big enough to fit a large chest size, the manufacturer assumed the coat needed to fit an even larger waist. He'd been hidden by an extra yard of white material yesterday. Not now.

He popped the last forkful in his mouth, set down his plate and pushed away from the counter. "The pan's already hot. They'll be ready in just a minute."

There was definitely no flab on that waist. She'd touched those six-pack abs.

"I like a girl with an appetite," he said, and she forced herself to stop ogling his body and look at his face instead. He was smiling.

What did he like? Oh—a girl with an appetite. She set her plate on the counter next to his. "I'll go ask Sophia how many more she wants, then."

His smile dimmed and he turned back to his frying pan. "She'll have to wait for the next batch. These are yours."

Once he shook them out of the pan and onto her plate, the weight of the iron skillet causing his biceps to flex in a rounded bulge, he didn't pour any more batter. He set the pan down, pushed his glasses up with one knuckle and walked the few steps to the entrance to the living room.

"Sophia, do you want any more pancakes?"

No answer.

"Sophia." Alex sounded more like a father speaking to a child than a man wooing a woman.

Grace hurried to smooth things over. "She probably didn't hear you."

Alex shot her a look that made her feel how weak her excuse was for her sister's rudeness. What had happened? Sophia had started the morning being nice to Alex while he'd iced her ankle. Usually, when her mood soured this suddenly, it meant she'd just gotten off the phone with Deezee. Surely, she hadn't been texting Deezee just now.

Sophia tossed her phone aside. "That screen is too small. Go get my iPad."

"Okay," Grace said. She started to duck around Alex, but he stopped her with a hand on her arm.

"Eat your pancakes first. They'll get cold."

"Oh." She looked from him to Sophia, not sure which one to listen to, but she'd been obeying Sophia far longer. "I know right where it is. Be back in one second."

She felt his disapproval when she returned with the iPad and handed it to her sister. She wished he hadn't seen Sophia's bossy side. Or maybe, she wished he hadn't seen her being so...subservient. She was just being a good assistant, making sure her boss had her devices when she needed them and where she needed them. Honestly, she was only practicing common decency, doing a small favor for someone with a badly sprained ankle. It was no big deal, any way one looked at it.

Then why did she feel like she'd been taken advantage of?

Alex came into the living room and handed her the plate. She gave him a lukewarm smile and ate some equally lukewarm pancakes.

Sophia could have phrased her request a little differently. *Hey, Gracie, when you're done eating, could you do me a favor and bring me my iPad?* Grace probably still would've gotten her the iPad immediately, but at least she wouldn't have looked like she was...inferior.

Subservient. Inferior.

She couldn't eat another bite.

"Martina will be here in a minute," Sophia said without taking her eyes off her screen. "Do we have any vodka?"

That snapped Grace out of her funk. She pulled her phone out of the back pocket of her jeans to check for messages from the publicist. "Martina's in town? She didn't call me to set up a meeting. What's this about?"

"Deezee. She'll make him straighten up."

Grace was stunned into silence. The publicist could spin a lot of mistakes, but not this. Deezee had been caught in a hotel with another woman. The damage had been done.

Grace knelt down to her sister's level. "Why?"

"She's coming because I called her."

Sophia had to know that wasn't what she'd been asking, but Grace didn't know how to start a real conversation with her anymore. At any rate, it would be wise to have Martina write some kind of statement for the press announcing that Sophia and Deezee were no longer a couple. But...

"Did Martina know he was going to be caught? Did she arrange it?"

"Are you crazy? This makes Deezee look bad. This makes me look bad."

"How else could she get here so soon from California?"

"She's in town for that South-by thing. There's a lot of people here."

Grace knew that *people* meant people who had power in the entertainment industry. *I told you it was a big event, but you didn't believe me.*

"So do we have vodka or what?"

Grace didn't look at Alex. She knew her cheeks were hot with embarrassment. "I don't know, Sophia. This isn't our house. Don't you think we ought to meet Martina at a restaurant or something?"

"No." Sophia was indignant, but at least she looked up from her screen. "For the amount of money we're paying her, she ought to come to me."

"Yes, but you can't host someone in a house that doesn't

belong to you. Alex might want to use his own house for something this morning. We might be in his way."

"I've got a cast on, for God's sake. I'm not going anywhere. I don't want to be photographed like this." She looked up from her phone to fix teary eyes on Grace. "Besides, it really hurts to walk, even with the boot on."

It was no use. Sophia had too many points to back up her obstinacy, and it was Grace who had to be flexible. She turned to Alex, forced to apologize for Sophia. "I'm so sorry about this. It's just one woman coming to talk business with Sophia, and she's already on her way. We'll try to keep it short. I didn't mean to invade your house on your day off."

Alex looked at her with those blue eyes for a long moment. "I know you didn't."

"Vodka," Sophia said.

I cannot believe I'm having to ask this.

"And do you happen to have any vodka on hand?"

Alex walked right past her and stood over Sophia. "I'm not serving you vodka. You're on pain medicine and antibiotics. Neither one goes well with alcohol."

Sophia tossed her hair back and looked up at him. "It's not for me. It's for my publicist. That's her trademark. She always has a vodka and tonic when she takes a meeting. And yes, before you say it, I know it's only nine in the morning. That's what makes it a memorable trademark."

Alex ran his hand over his bearded jaw in a move that looked like he was trying to restrain himself. Grace held her breath, afraid of the showdown that was surely coming.

Sophia capitulated. "You know what? We're not in public, so it's not like anyone will see her. Don't worry about the vodka."

"Thanks."

Grace could taste the sarcasm dripping from that one

word. Alex turned his back on Sophia. Grace thought he was headed for her, but he only passed her on the way to the master bedroom.

"I'll be in the shower," he muttered.

The bedroom door slammed before she could offer to clear her things out of his way. Quickly, she pictured how she'd left the bedroom. She'd left it neat enough, only her white pajamas lying across the bed. That shouldn't aggravate him any more than he already was.

Her tote bag was under the coffee table. She retrieved her notepad just as the doorbell rang.

"Get that."

Grace straightened abruptly. *Did you think I expected you to jump off the couch and hobble over there yourself?*

But she swallowed the sarcastic question. Maybe Alex could get away with it, but she never could. There was no sense in confronting Sophia, anyway. Once the Deezee effect wore off, her sister would stop being so rude and bossy.

The phase was over. It just didn't feel like it yet. But if Sophia didn't change her attitude soon, there would no longer be a question of whether or not Alex had a chance with her. Judging by this morning's exchange, it was Sophia who wouldn't have a chance with Alex.

What kind of sister would feel so hopeful about that?

Chapter Eleven

"What do you mean, he isn't going to apologize? He has to apologize."

Sophia's tantrum was directed at her publicist, but it was loud enough that Grace feared Alex could hear it through the walls and over the sound of running water in his shower.

"Don't yell at Martina." The words were out before Grace thought. Of course, Sophia would now do the opposite. It was rapidly becoming clear that Sophia was acting more like Deezee than ever, now that he'd cheated on her. Grace was baffled.

On cue, Sophia shouted, "I'll speak however I goddamned please."

Martina pointed at Sophia with her stylus. "Not when you are anywhere that anyone could possibly hit the record button on their cell phone. Your boyfriend could never get that through his thick head, and I'm washing my hands of him. You, I expect more from."

"You're firing Deezee?" Sophia was so aghast, she only seemed to have enough air to whisper.

"I fired him this morning. I don't keep clients that refuse my advice."

Sophia sat up a little straighter and set her phone aside.

Grace tried to keep a neutral expression on her face, a poker face like Alex, hoping no one could see how irritated she was with Martina's tactics. The publicist's ability to intimidate Sophia was useful, in its way. She'd kept Sophia from completely committing career suicide several times during the past three months, but Grace still didn't trust Martina.

Martina was the reason that Sophia had met Deezee this winter. Sophia and Grace had taken a week off in Telluride, a ski resort centered on a tiny Colorado mining town that was a haven for billionaires and A-list celebrities, one of whom had hired DJ Deezee Kalm to set up a rave in an old warehouse. Grace hadn't been enthralled by the neon lights and electronic dance music, so she'd stayed off the dance floor. So had Martina.

Within half an hour, Martina had found out for whom Grace was a personal assistant. The rest was history. Martina had introduced Sophia to the DJ that night, while he was in all his glory, standing on a stage and controlling a crowd with music. Martina had arranged for them to have an intimate lunch for two the next day in an excruciatingly expensive man-made snow cave. It had been money well spent. Now Martina was Sophia Jackson's publicist, as well.

That was Hollywood. Considering the way Grace had been befriended for an introduction and Deezee had practically been prostituted in order to achieve that goal, being Hollywood was awfully close to being Machiavellian.

"Couldn't you have released his apology before you fired him?" Sophia asked.

"Darling, when I fire a man, I refuse to spend another moment on him."

Grace wanted to set the record straight. As his publicist, Martina couldn't have fired Deezee: she was his employee. Martina might have decided not to work for him anymore, but that was *quitting*, and she'd quit when her client needed her most.

The *firing* verbiage worked on Sophia, though. She was blinded by the way Martina conducted herself, unable to see that it was Sophia's money, therefore it was Sophia's power. That was Hollywood, too.

"So what are we going to do?" When she didn't know she was the boss, Sophia pouted and whined like a child to get her way. "I don't wanna look like a loser. Everyone is laughing at me."

Thank goodness Alex wasn't in the room to hear this. Whiney Sophia wasn't necessarily preferable to Bossy Sophia.

"We will do nothing," Martina said. "Rumors die more quickly when you don't respond."

"I have to say nothing?" Sophia sounded like a kid saying *I have to eat broccoli?* "It's not a rumor when there are photos."

The sound of water running in the shower stopped. If they didn't get a plan together and conclude this meeting, Alex was going to witness everything. Despite the modern feel of his house, the 1930s floor plan had been preserved, and houses hadn't been built very large in the 1930s. The kitchen was separated from them by a wall, but there was a pass-through to the little dining area, which connected to this living room. He'd have to share this space with them, unless he stayed in the bathroom for a very, very long while.

Sophia took up the entire couch to keep her cast boot elevated, of course. Martina had enthroned herself in the large armchair. That left Grace to use one of the little dinette chairs. She'd carried it over to the couch, so she could sit next to Sophia. She ought to bring one over for Alex soon. She didn't think he was a man who'd hide in his own bedroom.

"We have to come up with something for me to say," Sophia said. "Have you read the comments on the photos? Everyone is wondering how bad I must be in bed if Deezee would cheat on someone who looks like me with someone who looks like her. Fix this."

Martina, her dark red lips forming a displeased line at receiving an order, clipped her stylus to her tablet.

Sophia froze, not even daring to cough, clearly afraid Martina was about to fire her. Grace held her breath, too, but she felt something closer to hope than fear. Sophia didn't seem to be actually sad about losing Deezee, and if they could lose Martina, as well...

"After all, you're the best publicist in the industry." Sophia spoke the hyperbole meekly, then lapsed into her anxious silence.

With her audience suitably subdued, Martina spoke. "We can release a statement. You'll say that of course you've seen the photos, but they don't concern you. It was never serious between you and Deezee."

Grace's patience ran out. She didn't want to be abusing Alex's hospitality with this meeting. She didn't want Alex to hear her sister whining. Most of all, she didn't want to stay silent while Martina gave her sister bad advice in return for good money.

"No one will believe it was never serious," Grace said.

"Sophia and Deezee were photographed kissing at the beach the day before yesterday. You made sure of it."

Sophia looked at her like she was a table lamp that had suddenly offered an opinion.

Remember when you used to ask my opinion on everything, Sophia?

Sophia reached for Grace's arm. "Remind me. Which outlets showed those beach photos?"

Grace kept a list on her own tablet device, of course, along with screen shots whenever she spotted her sister on gossip blogs and entertainment media. With Martina glaring daggers at her, Grace dropped her gaze to her tote bag, which was still sitting under the coffee table. She'd have to literally bow down before Sophia and Martina to reach it and retrieve her tablet.

She heard the bedroom door open. Alex would walk in as she was crawling. *Subservient. Inferior.*

She made no move toward her tote bag. Instead, she looked back at Martina, and hoped her poker face wasn't as nonexistent as Alex had said it was. "Let's look at your list of the media outlets you were successful with."

After a long moment, Martina unclipped her stylus once more. "Of course. This is what I'm here for."

This is what we pay you for.

Sophia gave Grace a little pat, then slowly rolled her booted foot from left to right as she listened to Martina's list. Grace watched the motion with pleasure; that pat had felt like sisterly approval.

Alex must have passed behind her on his way to the kitchen, for she heard the sound of a drawer opening, the rattle of silverware. She guessed he was putting away the breakfast dishes.

"Obviously, then, everyone knows we were serious. Pretending we weren't won't fix this." Sophia sounded more like the pre-Deezee version of herself. No whining, thank goodness.

"I'll come up with a way for you to get the most mile-age out of this bad publicity." Martina tapped her stylus on her tablet at the same rapid pace that she tapped her spiked heel on the polished concrete floor.

We didn't need anyone to handle bad publicity until you brought bad publicity into our lives.

The kitchen sounds had stopped. Grace peeked over her shoulder. Alex was sitting down at the dinette table with his back to them, intent on a newspaper. He was being so polite, giving them a sense of privacy, but he had to be able to hear every word.

Martina's stylus and her heel both went still. "The mys-tery is this trip to Texas. You're dropping out of the public eye for a week. Why? We can spin it so that you left Hol-lywood to visit a hot new lover in Texas. You abandoned Deezee, you see. You left first. If you'd already found an-other man *before* last night, then this girl becomes noth-ing more than his rebound girl. She's a consolation prize, or a woman Deezee was only using to assuage the pain of *his* broken heart."

"And she's so hideous, the fact that he went from some-one like me to someone like her will make him look des-perate."

Grace cringed. When she and Alex had talked on that bench yesterday, she'd bragged about her sister's lack of snobbery.

"What do you think, Grace?"

Her sister was actually asking for her input. It felt like it had been years instead of months since she'd been treated like a part of her sister's team instead of her sister's er-rand girl.

Martina steamrolled over Grace's chance to offer her

opinion. "It's the best option. You stay hidden, and I'll let it be known that you are not to be expected to attend any South-by events, because you're on something of a honeymoon with your new man."

Grace glanced at Alex's back again. Had he heard Sophia ask for her advice? She wanted him to believe what she'd told him yesterday, that her sister was a good person and a hard worker who deserved her success—and who deserved Grace's loyalty.

"I think a fake boyfriend is a dangerous idea." Grace scooted her chair so that she was facing Sophia more squarely. "You know what they say. If there's no photo, it didn't happen. Eventually, when no photos of a mystery man in Texas surface, you'll end up looking desperate, so desperate that you made up a fake boyfriend. Don't risk it. Your reputation always was that you're smart and mature."

"Was?" Only Sophia could put so many nuances of emotion in that one syllable.

"That's why it caused a sensation when you started dating Deezee. He wasn't the kind of guy people expected Sophia Jackson to date."

"It was a brilliant move," Martina said. "It got you tons of exposure."

It was time for Grace to do some steamrolling herself. "Dating him changed your public image, but not for the better. If the industry is already less confident that you are the smart and mature actress they thought you were, then imagine what will happen to you if word gets out that you made up a whole fake boyfriend scenario. Professionally, it could be a disaster."

Sophia looked from her to Martina. "Grace is right."

Grace is right.

Grace's hands were shaking again. Thanks to Alex's pancakes, she knew it wasn't low blood sugar. It was sheer relief. She'd just fought for her sister's career against an experienced publicist, and she'd won. She sat back, sagging in relief as much as she could in a hard chair.

Martina stood and began pacing. "Then we need to arrange for you to be seen. That hideous boot comes off in a week, correct?"

"I'll still have to wear an ankle wrap." Sophia shot a look at Alex's back. "And the doctor says no high heels for two more weeks after that."

Martina checked her tablet without slowing her steps. "There's a black-tie event put on by a few oh-so-worthy causes toward the end of South-by. A charity gala. Tell your stylist you need one of those hems that puddles on the ground, so no one will see you're wearing flats."

Grace picked up her trusty notebook. It was time to make a list and get this meeting adjourned, so Alex wouldn't have to politely ignore people in his own house any longer.

"I'll contact the stylist," she said. "The messaging is everything. We need a gown that a smart and mature woman would wear who wasn't pining after a cheating boyfriend. It shouldn't look desperate, like she's trying too hard. Something that says she's confident being out in public alone."

"Alone?" Sophia and Martina both looked at her like she was a bizarre talking table lamp again.

"She needs to be seen with a new man, so it's not just a rumor," Martina said. "She'll be a surprise celebrity at the event, and she'll have a surprise boyfriend on her arm. This will solve the mystery of why she's disappeared in Texas. The press will eat it up."

"What man do you have in mind?" Sophia asked. "Is there anyone still in the closet who'd like to appear devoted to me?"

Grace didn't dare turn around to see Alex's reaction to that. She spoke as quietly as she could to her sister. "I thought you said I was right about avoiding the fake boyfriend?"

"You were right that rumors about a fake boyfriend weren't enough. We need an actual man for photos, someone who is here in Texas to justify why I flew down in the first place, *before* Deezee cheated on me."

Martina gestured toward the flat-screen television, as if she could bring its black, powered-off screen to life with a dramatic flourish of her hands. "I can see the gossip shows now. 'Sophia Jackson has a secret rendezvous in Austin.' A classy gown, a handsome mystery man. It will sink Deezee and his tawdry hotel girl. Sink him."

She was totally focused on defeating the man who'd once been her most famous client. He'd only been a stepping stone to Sophia.

Grace gave up trying to look bold. "Deezee is going to be angry. He's unpredictable when he's angry."

Sophia dropped her head back on the couch, looking tired. "Well, then, we need someone brave enough to weather his crap. Better yet, we need someone who won't care if Deezee goes on a rant about him."

Grace doodled in a corner of her notebook. "Someone with no reputation left to save? I don't think you should be paired with another loose cannon."

Martina stopped next to Grace. "Sophia means someone who isn't in the industry at all. Deezee couldn't hurt someone who didn't need to impress the press."

And you wouldn't have to deal with another celebrity's angry publicist, would you?

Sophia had her eyes closed now, pneumonia wiping her out. "It's hard to find someone who isn't in the industry. Grace had a point about reviving that smart and mature approach, although *mature* is the absolutely wrong word to use."

"Let's say *down-to-earth*, shall we?" Martina said. "We need someone normal. An everyday man, making Sophia Jackson seem approachable, someone women identify with. Someone men think they might actually stand a chance with."

Sophia opened one eye. "But Mr. Normal Guy will have to be attractive. Hard body. Not old."

Grace glanced over her shoulder. Alex was still sitting with his back to them. His hair was damp from his shower, almost black against the nape of his neck, longer than it had looked at the hospital. He wore a red T-shirt that was so worn, it had faded to a pinkish mud color. He looked down-to-earth to her. Not old. And last night, in the light of the refrigerator, he'd definitely had a hard body.

Martina kept talking. "So, we need a man who is respectably employed but not tycoon-wealthy who lives here in Texas who is the right age and who is straight and single and willing to pretend he's dating Sophia Jackson. And we need to find him today, tomorrow at the latest."

A moment of silence followed that.

This is my sister. I have to try one more time.

Grace clenched her notepad in her hands. "Or we could try the truth. Deezee was a lousy boyfriend, which you found out when you flew down for the Texas Rescue grand-opening ceremony."

No one answered her. Behind her, she heard Alex shove his chair away from the table.

Martina was glued to her tablet screen now, as obsessed as Sophia usually was with her phone. "This black-tie event benefits several causes, including Texas Rescue. Absolutely perfect. Your trip begins and ends with a Texas

Rescue event, and you'll have a secret getaway with a hot guy in the middle."

Grace felt Alex's presence behind her. Martina did a little double take when she looked from her tablet to the man standing behind Grace's chair.

"Alex," he said over Grace's head, the briefest of introductions. "I live here. If you're referring to next week's Black and White Ball, it's sold out."

"They won't turn Sophia Jackson away."

He addressed her sister directly. "You can have my ticket if you need it. West Central is one of the beneficiaries, as well. Part of the proceeds are going to help replace those curtains in the ER with walls. I'm sure you'll want to help make it a success."

Sophia opened both eyes then. "Like I care. I'm never going to be your patient again."

"Glad to hear it."

Grace wasn't sure how to interpret that. Maybe he meant that he was glad Sophia wasn't his patient, because he couldn't date a patient.

Martina dismissed Alex with a flick of her fingers. "There is no question that she can go to the ball. Now we just have to pick out which guy she should take." She sat down on the armrest of the couch, nestling right next to Sophia, like they were sisters about to share a Netflix marathon on her tablet.

Grace had to scoot her chair closer to the sofa to be able to see the screen, as well. Alex was behind her still. It would take more than Martina's finger flick to make him move if he didn't feel like it.

Martina ignored them, cozy with her client. "The only positive photos of you on social media for the past three months were taken with Texas Rescue yesterday."

I arranged that photo op.

No one thanked her.

"Let's review that ribbon-cutting group photo." Martina pointed at the screen. "How about him?"

Of course, she'd pointed at the most obviously handsome guy. Grace shook her head. "Thor? He's not interested in Sophia."

Sophia roused herself, offended. "Says who?"

"You didn't like him, either. He's the paramedic that actually rode with you in the back of the ambulance."

"Oh, him. I'm an actress. I can pretend I like him."

Martina had already moved on. "There are three firefighters. This one is too young."

Grace felt Alex step closer behind her. On top of everything else, she now had to suffer while he listened to her sister sort through all his friends like they were her personal shopping catalog. This wasn't going to put Sophia in her best light.

"This one's too old," Sophia announced.

Charming, Sis. Just charming.

Martina tilted her head and considered the photo. "But very distinguished. A little Clooney gray at the temples. He could add some gravitas to your reputation."

"Too old." Sophia tapped the last fireman with her fingernail. "This one's just right. Looks about thirty. Confident. Photographs well."

Alex bent so close, Grace could feel the rumble of his deep voice as he spoke over her shoulder. "That's Luke. He's married to the director of Texas Rescue."

"Buzz kill," Sophia muttered, as if Alex had arranged for this Luke to be married just to spoil her day.

"How about one of the doctors?" Martina asked. "They get instant respect as soon as you say their name. Imagine yourself saying 'I'm here with Dr. John Doe from Texas Rescue.' This one looks perfect."

"All those guys are married and happy about it. Some of the women in that photo are single, though." Alex sounded a little sarcastic to Grace's ear.

Martina set the tablet in her lap. "Here's a story. 'Sophia Jackson has a female fling, a girlfriend with benefits, taking a break after all the drama of dating men, most recently DJ Deezee Kalm.' We could work that angle."

Alex stood up straight again, leaving Grace's shoulder feeling cold. "You don't decide to change your sexual orientation for a week. That's not how it works."

"It's called experimentation," Martina said, sounding condescending. "Very Bohemian and naughty in my day, but now it's almost *de rigueur.* Still, if any of these women were inclined…"

Grace hated her blush, but she hated even more that Alex was witnessing this. They were in his house, though. She couldn't ask him to leave his own living room.

"I want to be seen with a man," Sophia said. "Thirty-ish. A doctor would work."

They were describing Alex. He was standing right here. It wasn't like either woman to beat around the bush, but maybe they were hoping he'd volunteer.

"It sounds like you're talking about Alex," she said, wanting to get this over with. "Dr. Alex Gregory."

Sophia dismissed her with a wave of her hand. "The man has to be drop-dead gorgeous to make it believable that I'd leave Deezee for him."

Grace felt all the pain of that insult, but more, the unfairness of it. She dared to turn her head far enough to see how Alex was taking it. He was really very handsome underneath all that scruffy…

Oh, my.

All that scruffiness was gone. Alex had shaved. His

136 HER TEXAS RESCUE DOCTOR

hair, still wet from the shower, was slicked back. With those dark-framed glasses…

Martina had twisted around, too, and was openly studying Alex. "Actually, he's got a very Clark Kent vibe going."

Grace's breath caught—it was what she'd thought from the first.

Martina tapped her stylus. "Which means we could turn him into Superman."

Sophia slid farther down the couch, settling in for a nap. "Be serious."

"I am," Martina said, her voice as sharp as the points of her designer pumps. "Open your eyes, Sophia."

She obeyed, craning her neck to check out her host. "Oh."

"*Oh*, indeed. Clark turned into Superman in seconds, but thankfully, we've got a whole week." Martina stood and tossed her tablet on the couch. "Well, I'm positively parched. Someone get me a vodka tonic."

No one moved.

Grace couldn't stop staring at clean-shaven Alex, but his neutral expression was impossible to read.

"He hasn't agreed to anything, Martina," she said.

Martina only laughed. "Well, Dr. Gregory, are you ready to become the most interesting man in Texas?"

Chapter Twelve

"No."

Alex crossed his arms over his chest, refusing to cower or cringe as three women evaluated him solely on his looks. He knew how to act like he didn't care: tall kids who wore glasses and spoke with Russian accents had to learn quickly in high school.

"That's all you have to say?" The woman named Martina looked exactly as he expected a behind-the-scenes show business shark to look. She was what he'd expected Sophia's assistant to be. "I'm offering you the chance to walk the red carpet with one of America's hottest stars, and all you can say is no?"

"No, thank you."

"Very funny."

At least Martina got his sarcasm.

He looked at Grace, the voice of reason in this group. Her knuckles were nearly white as she clutched her notebook. He hated to see her so anxious. She'd done such a good job defending her sister and taking on Martina, even if she'd lost the battle over this publicity stunt.

"Do you have someone in your life, then?" Martina persisted. "Someone you're afraid to make jealous?"

"No."

"You'll be compensated for your time away from work, of course. I hear those med-school student loans are such a burden. Young doctors are drowning in debt, they say."

The loans weren't fun, certainly, but a substantial portion of his medical school had been covered by scholarships. As Chief Resident during his last year, he'd earned a higher salary than the other young doctors-in-training. His house was the right size for a bachelor. He had one high-end pickup truck and two carbon-fiber road bikes. He was doing just fine.

Ms. Hollywood Shark was taking the wrong path to persuade him. The day he paid off a med-school loan by dressing up as a starlet's boy toy was the day he needed to turn in his man card.

Grace was looking at him with that same look she'd had in the ER's kitchen. Fear, worry—and hope. She was facing a mess, and she hoped he'd be able to help her fix it.

Of course, anything that hurt Sophia's acting career would hurt Grace, too. That was unfortunate, but still not a reason to make him play their game. This entire conversation had only driven home the point that an actress's life was inherently self-absorbed. He didn't feel obligated to support that.

"Grace will arrange your clothing," Martina decreed. "I don't know how much a personal trainer can do in a week, but try."

He had a landscape project to finish this week. The only

thing he could use a personal trainer for was as an extra set of hands to haul wheelbarrows of gravel.

"A haircut. A facial. Spray tan. I expect him to be able to dance," Sophia said between coughs that sounded fractionally better than yesterday's.

Grace spoke to her sister. "You don't sound like you'll be dancing a week from today." Then she looked to him, trusting him to have the answers. "Will she?"

"It's possible, at least for a song or two, if she doesn't do anything crazy. Shortness of breath or pain in the ankle are pretty obvious signs it's time to stop."

"I'll be ready. Get him dance lessons. Be sure the photographers are told ahead of time to expect me to dance. It's the easiest way to make a couple look more romantically involved than they are."

Grace opened her notebook and started writing.

Something inside him snapped. Grace was Sophia's personal assistant, and that meant she'd execute this fake boyfriend plan to the best of her ability, whether she agreed with it or not. Whether Sophia appreciated her hard work or not.

Whether he was the fake boyfriend or not.

He'd advised her to find a new job, but she'd explained that her boss was her sister, as if that made it okay for her to put up with being treated badly. *Family.* Sometimes, a family member could calm a frightened patient, but it was just as likely that the family member made the problem worse, like a father who pushed his son to play soccer the day after an injury. *Family* made people stay in bad situations, even when it was a family member who hurt them and caused them pain. People like Mrs. Burns.

His mother.

Grace.

He walked around the couch and looked out the sliding

glass doors, letting his focus settle on the shapes of the cactus he'd protected throughout a freezing winter. Behind him, Martina took a phone call as Sophia continued to dictate the list of her wants and needs. He stared at his cactus and tuned them out.

He wasn't being logical about this. He couldn't equate Grace's situation with women who'd been physically hurt by the family members who supposedly loved them. There was no assault and battery. Grace was in no physical danger here.

He turned around to watch her writing with her white-knuckled grip on her pen, hunched in her hard chair while the others lounged on upholstery, and he felt a quiet fury all the same. Of all the people in this room, only one was anxious and stressed and unhappy. The one who wanted the best for someone who didn't care how she felt in return. The one who was expected to do the most work and sit in the least comfortable chair.

That one was Grace. There was no violence, but Alex recognized other similarities. She was kept in line with scraps of attention. She was ignored until any reasonable person would leave, and then thrown an almost-apology. *I really took it out on you—we didn't know I had pneumonia, though, did we?* She was condescendingly allowed to have made a good point. *Grace had a point—although* mature *is the absolutely wrong word to use.* It was just enough to keep Grace hoping that if she stayed a little longer, her sister would treat her better. *It won't happen again.*

How could he make Grace see how warped that pattern was? Her job and her family were making her miserable. She ought to be doing something she found more rewarding, whatever that might be. As it was, she was so busy running and fetching that he doubted she'd had the chance to be alone with her own thoughts. She needed time to evaluate where she was and where she wanted to be.

He could give that to her.

He spoke to the group as a whole. "I haven't agreed to escort Sophia to the Black and White Ball."

Sophia stopped whining. Martina stopped texting.

Alex spoke evenly, without emotion, as he'd been doing since childhood. "As you said, my time is valuable."

"Which is why we'll pay you," Martina replied. "You'll be allowed to keep the clothing, as well. Any jewelry will have to returned, of course."

"I have commitments during my days off work which I can't ignore. If I have to spend time preparing for your project, then I'll need someone to spend time on my projects in return. I want to be paid for my time by being given time."

"You want me to visit the hospital, whoop-de-doo." Sophia managed to sound both vain and world-weary at the same time.

"I want Grace's time in return for my own."

"Grace's?" Sophia tipped over, going from sitting to horizontal on the couch. "Okay, fine. I don't care. It's a deal."

"It isn't your deal to make, Sophia. If Grace agrees, then you and I need to clarify that if Grace is working with me, then she won't be around to fetch and carry for you. I don't want her to work any more hours than she already does. Once she puts in eight or nine hours in a day, whether it's with me or with you, she's done."

"Whatever. I'm so effing tired, I just want to sleep."

He walked around the couch to stand before Grace and held out his hand for a formal shake. "I'm willing to give you my time if you're willing to give me yours. Do we have an agreement?"

It was a simple deal. Sophia would get what she wanted. Martina would get what she wanted. There was no risk that anything would happen to him other than getting a haircut and a tuxedo. Simple.

Hope returned to Grace's angelic face, and she placed her hand in his, confident that he'd solved all her problems, unaware that he had ulterior motives. He intended to help Grace change her life.

Alex felt a twinge of guilt. A woman who lived in Hollywood ought to know that life was only this simple in the movies.

Grace was simply delighted.

Everything was going according to plan. It seemed like it had been ages since she'd looked out a van window and wished her sister would fall in love with a nice, normal guy from Texas Rescue.

As if she'd been granted three wishes, everything was coming true. Overnight, Deezee had been eliminated from their lives. Alex had volunteered to date her sister. And Sophia—

Well, Sophia wasn't showing much interest in Alex yet. Martina had actually taken more notice of him. *And I can't stop staring at him.*

She wouldn't dwell on that. This was about saving Sophia. Her sister had only cried over Deezee for a short time before fury had set in, but her heart couldn't have hardened between eating pancakes and having a meeting with Martina. When Deezee realized how much he'd lost, he might come crawling back. Sophia might still want him, and they'd be right back where they'd started.

Grace couldn't let that happen. Alex was the key. If Sophia fell for Alex, then Deezee couldn't suck her sister back into his dysfunctional world. Grace had one week to turn Alex into the perfect man for her sister.

At least she didn't have to try to turn Sophia into the perfect woman for Alex. All morning, Grace had been worried that Alex would be totally turned off by the calculations and machinations that were necessary to keep Sophia's career and reputation intact, but apparently, Alex had overlooked it. He'd volunteered to be her fake boyfriend, despite it all.

He agreed to help Sophia by spending time with me.

It would be foolish to feel flattered. She was Grace the Assistant. Grace the Sister.

"Grace?"

"Yes?"

"I'm taking another meeting." Martina headed for the door, moving fast on those stilettos.

"Wait—we need to work out the details."

But Martina didn't slow down, so Grace jumped up to follow her, notebook at the ready. "You'll get the tickets to the ball, right?"

Martina flicked her fingers. "You handle this, Grace. I'm the idea man. You're the one who makes it happen. *Ciao.*"

Grace clenched her notebook as Martina slammed the door.

"Is it safe?" Alex murmured behind her. "Is she gone?"

Grace turned around, feeling foolish for running after Martina.

Alex didn't step back. "You know, Martina was exactly what I expected you to be. Before you got to the ER, your sister had been threatening me with her fearsome assistant. She said you were going to straighten everything out."

Grace couldn't remember ever being told that Sophia had talked about her when she wasn't around. What an odd thing for Sophia to have done, threatening a doctor with her.

"I can't imagine why she thought I'd be able to get her the hospital room she wanted."

"You help her get everything she wants."

Grace hesitated. Had that been a compliment, or a criticism?

"That's my job," she said, watching him closely for a response.

He studied her in return. "That is your job, isn't it?"

Grace looked toward the couch. She was pretty sure Sophia was sleeping through this conversation. Well, her sister had pneumonia. She was supposed to be sleeping right now; that was her job. Sophia had to look smart and mature—no, down-to-earth—and unaffected by the antics of an LA disc jockey when she appeared at the Texas Rescue benefit in one week. In order to pull that off, she needed to get healthy. And she needed Alex.

Which meant Grace had a job to do.

It was time to turn Alex into the perfect man for her sister.

Chapter Thirteen

Grace had never felt less motivated to do her job in her entire life.

Her three wishes had been granted, and the rest was up to her. She'd wished they could stay in Texas. She'd wished for Deezee to disappear from their lives. But that third wish...

She's wished for a good man for Sophia. He was standing right here, and it was up to Grace to bring them together.

"Sophia's asleep. Let's get a cup of coffee and go on the porch." Alex was already halfway in the kitchen as he spoke. "You take it black, right?"

He remembered.

She shouldn't be so surprised. After all, they'd just had breakfast an hour ago. But he'd paid attention to a little detail about her, and it gave her a thrill to know she'd been noticed.

Being in the tight confines of the galley kitchen with him brought up memories of midnight. She had to squash them down; this was her sister's new fake boyfriend, and if wishes came true, he'd become a real boyfriend.

She took her coffee and skirted around the couch to the sliding glass door. Alex stayed right behind her, reaching around her, opening the door. As she stepped onto the patio, her long hair caught on his hand, producing the gentlest tug behind her ear.

She might as well be that woman in a historical movie, she felt so very *aware*. Had her hair brushed him accidentally, or had he touched her on purpose?

If she could have a fourth wish...

Oh, that would be so easy. She'd wish that Alex was hers. She'd stop pretending she didn't notice him. No more tentative touches. She'd turn and bury her hand in the thick, dark hair at the nape of his neck and pull him close.

Why not?

Alex set his coffee on the patio table. "I'll be right back."

He went into the living room, took a folded blanket from a shelf and shook it out, blue-and-silver sports team colors looking bright in the sun that poured in the window. As she watched, he lifted it above the couch and let it fall softly, naturally, over her sleeping sister.

Sitting in the warm sunshine, with her hands wrapped around a mug of hot coffee, Grace felt her heart freeze.

She hadn't seen anyone take care of her sister like that, not in ten years. Not since they'd lost their parents in one horrible blow, forcing Sophia to be the oldest, the breadwinner, the decision-maker. Sure, Grace might fetch her coffee, but only when Sophia told her to. Hair and makeup artists might fuss over her, but Sophia paid them. The studios, the agents, the publicist—they all wanted something from the bankable commodity that was Sophia Jackson.

Only Alex, wonderful Alex, was tall and strong and confident enough to treat Sophia like a person, not like a money-making celebrity. He was nice to her, despite having seen her at her worst. Because he wasn't in awe of Sophia, because he didn't depend on Sophia, he was just what Sophia needed.

That's why not.

Grace sat at the table and took a deep breath, forcing the air past the stone in her chest, expanding her ribs despite that sharp pain of jealousy. She'd wished for this. She'd wished that her sister could meet a man like Alex, and she had.

She would pull off this transformation, and Sophia would notice Alex. More than that, she'd make sure Alex knew how great Sophia was, too.

Alex sat down on her side of the patio table. Their chairs were side by side, so close that she could feel his body heat. Her heart began to thaw.

I wish I didn't want you so much.

Pen poised over the blank paper, she waited until she was sure her breathing was steady. Then she looked up at Alex. "What traits do you look for in a woman?"

He raised a brow. "That's your first question? I thought you might ask me what jacket size I need for the tuxedo. I've already rented one, by the way."

She forced a smile and turned the page, titling it *Clothes*. "If you tell me where you rented it, I'll cancel it. The maker of Sophia's gown will probably have an agreement with a menswear designer. They'll send a tailor to fit you."

"You're not my secretary. I'll cancel it myself if I have to. Let's wait and see if it's really necessary."

"It will be. If Sophia wears Lauren, for example, then

you'll be expected to wear a Lauren tux, as well. It's all contractual." She felt steadier on this familiar ground, speaking about the workings of her Hollywood life. Her heart could remain cold, indifferent.

Alex took off his glasses and set them on the table, then kicked back in his chair and contemplated the porch ceiling for a moment. "How about your gown? Will you coordinate with Sophia, or do you get to choose your own color and style?" He turned blue eyes on her.

Oh, so blue—vivid and naked, with no glasses adding a layer of safety. Grace swallowed hard. "I'm not on the red carpet, so I don't need a gown. Um—do you have to wear your glasses? Do you have contacts?"

One eyebrow rose again. "Do my glasses have to be a particular designer when I stand next to your sister?"

"We'll get you new frames. But if you can get by without the glasses at all… Sometimes the cameras catch a reflection, and then people wouldn't get to see your—" She was blushing, darn it. Warm cheeks, cold heart. "You and Sophia would look striking together. You both have such blue eyes."

She couldn't quite look into his. She dropped her gaze. Under that loose, faded shirt, his biceps were tight and tan. Her heart didn't feel so frozen.

Alex was quiet, so she peeked up at him.

"You're not afraid Sophia and I will look too much like brother and sister with our matching eye color? That's not a turnoff?"

"Blue eyes are never a turnoff."

"I'm glad to hear that."

Had he meant that he was glad *she* wasn't turned off? As if.

She felt antsy, edgy. If he and Sophia actually got married, he'd be her brother. She didn't want such a hot brother.

The Thor paramedic guy would've been fine, but Alex? No way.

She needed to stay focused on the task at hand. That was what her lists were for. She jotted *cancel tux* and *eyeglass frames*, then turned back to the previous blank page. "Let's get back to the first question. What do you look for in the ideal woman?"

"I'm taking Sophia to this event whether she's my ideal woman or not."

Grace needed to know, anyway. If there was some trait that Alex liked and Sophia already had, then Grace intended to emphasize it. If there was anything she could do to make Sophia more appealing to Alex, she'd do it. Her cold heart would let her be ruthless. Someone like him wasn't going to cross their paths again.

"You can just smile and pose for photos as you enter the venue, but there will be press asking you questions all night. You have to remember that when you are part of a celebrity's life, you are on the record every single second, with every single person, not just reporters. You have to be very careful about talking to people."

"I'm not going to talk about Sophia with strangers. We'll be sitting with people I know from Texas Rescue."

"You still have to guard what you say. My dry cleaner has been asked by a blogger if I told him anything new about Sophia. The clerk at the deli counter has been asked which sandwich I ordered for myself, so he could figure out that the other one was for Sophia. She likes turkey, dry, on whole wheat with sprouts, by the way."

He'd started frowning. When it was just the two of them, she realized, he didn't keep that poker face in place. "I think the guys in Texas Rescue are going to be a little more loyal to me than a deli counter clerk is to you."

"They can be your loyal friends, but they'll still be

grilled. You can't slip when you talk to them, so they won't slip if they talk to a reporter. We have to prepare. It's like that movie *Green Card.* Do you know it?"

"I can't imagine how my life is like a movie."

"It's one of the standards in the industry, a marriage-of-convenience story that came out twenty-five years ago. Gérard Depardieu, Andie MacDowell. It was a rom-com—that means romantic comedy—but it still got an Academy Award nomination, which is unusual."

"And this has to do with my ideal woman?"

"It has to do with telling me your preferences. In the movie, the marriage began as a sham to get him a green card, but then the man and woman had to get to know one another in order to pass government interviews, sort of like how you'll have to pass reporters' interviews. They memorized each other's wants and likes to make their fake relationship seem real. And, of course, once they got to know each other, they ended up really falling in love."

Love. The word seemed to linger in the air, suspended between the warm coffee and his blue eyes.

He looked away first. "You know your movies."

She shrugged, just one shoulder. "I guess you could say it's part of my job. I'm in the industry, sort of."

The frown deepened. "You are definitely in the industry. Sophia Jackson wouldn't be the success she is without you."

"You don't know her very well yet. She's driven. She's the one who won't waste her time reading a rom-com script unless someone says it's *Green Card* caliber. The last few months with Deezee were really an aberration. She's normally very focused."

"She can focus on her career because you save her so much time and distraction. This morning, from what I heard, you know the industry as well as she does. That's why she asks for your advice."

He'd noticed. Grace had hoped it would make her look better in his eyes, but that was before she'd seen how tender he was toward her sister.

Had she misread that? As the blanket had floated down over her sister, Alex had looked...not exactly tender, actually. Perhaps he'd looked sort of matter-of-fact about it all. There was a person with pneumonia who might feel chilled while she slept, so he put a blanket on her. That didn't mean he was falling in love, did it?

It would by the time she was through with it. Alex was about to learn everything good there was to know about Sophia.

"She could hire a hundred different people to be her assistant, but you couldn't hire anyone to be Sophia Jackson. I only know the year *Green Card* was released because it was the same year I was born."

"So you're twenty-five."

"Yes." Her pen hovered over the paper. "How old are you?"

"Thirty-one.

"Perfect. Sophia is twenty-nine."

"You're writing down my age?"

"I'll make a list of things Sophia should know about you. She'll memorize it. She has an amazing memory. When she's filming, she memorizes pages of script every night. Sometimes, the writers will change the dialog and hand her new pages in the morning, and she'll know them by her first call. You'll see. I'll type up the notes I take this morning, and she'll know you inside and out by tomorrow."

"Or, she and I could have a normal conversation on the way to the ball."

"I wouldn't be a very good personal assistant if I let you two get into the limo unprepared."

"The limo? I take it I'm not driving." He held up a hand to forestall her. "I'm sure there's a good reason for that. What else do you want to know?"

He rested his forearms on the table, leaning toward the serenity garden that was his backyard, but he didn't look at the cactus and fruit trees. Instead, he looked at her. It was amazing what a difference a shave made. A few good photos of those sky blue eyes, and the public would have no doubts that Sophia Jackson had spent the week in Texas *not* being heartbroken over DJ Deezee Kalm. Anyone who pitied Sophia this morning would envy her once she made her appearance with Alex.

Grace wrote *Preferences* at the top of her page.

"I don't have a list," Alex said. "How can I order up a human being to my specifications?"

"You could start with the basics, like blue eyes and blond hair."

"I've never had a thing for any particular coloring." He let his gaze roam over her, as if he was seriously considering her coloring.

Beige, boring, blushing...

His voice grew quieter. "But I'm definitely not immune to beauty. When a woman is really beautiful, it doesn't matter if she's dressed up or dressed down or...wearing her pajamas."

That was Sophia. No plastic surgery, no Botox, no fillers. Thank goodness Deezee had self-destructed before he could convince her to change anything.

"I'll tell you something else I notice," Alex said. "I admire a woman who isn't afraid to stand up for what is right. Loyalty to her friends and family is very appealing."

He was describing Sophia perfectly. Grace jotted down *loyalty, ethics, beauty*.

"It's too bad we can't use the whole story when you're asked how you two met. If you could tell everyone how you were impressed with her loyalty yesterday, that would be something unique."

"When was this?" He sounded genuinely curious.

"At the hotel, when she encouraged me to talk to the police. She knew that writing that witness statement was the right thing to do. It seemed to me that you liked her a little more after that."

He sat back, which made his shoulder brush hers. "It was nice to see that you were getting some support from her. *You* were the one doing the right thing."

Grace angled her chair toward him. It allowed her to face him more fully. It also kept their shoulders from touching. "You two have so much in common, see? You came to the hotel to support me, too. You both want to see justice served."

"That's one way to look at it."

Grace counted it as a small victory.

Alex seemed impatient. "We can't bring police statements into this. Everything with Mrs. Burns is confidential. We should stick to our initial contact. It's simple and it's true. I met Sophia when she came into the emergency room with a suspected fracture."

"And what was your first impression?"

"An X-ray would be necessary."

Grace stared at him for a second.

He hadn't made a joke, so she tried not to laugh, but a little snort of amusement bubbled out of her, anyway. "You can't be such a doctor with the press, okay? When someone asks you what your first impression of Sophia was—"

She couldn't finish her sentence because she was trying

too hard not to laugh. "I'm sorry. I just—it's just—that is the least romantic answer a man has ever given."

This time, his raised brow was accompanied by a little duck of his chin. The calm and confident Dr. Gregory looked a little sheepish. And adorable.

Was it okay to think of a brother as adorable?

Grace got her giggles under control. "We've got a lot of work to do. Don't worry, I won't let you down."

"I'm sure you won't let anyone down. I think you're almost too good at your job. Don't let anyone treat you like you're easy to replace."

The last of Grace's laughter died. Easy to replace? Had Martina said that? Sophia?

Alex put his glasses back on. "I'm so confident that you'll get your job done that I think we can stop here and move on to my project."

When he stood and held out his hand for hers, she was curious enough to forget that touching him was off-limits. She placed her hand in his, and he pulled her to her feet.

"You never told me what your project was," she said.

"Come for a ride with me and find out."

Chapter Fourteen

Alex thought he was a good doctor. He was a strong cyclist. He was proud of the way he designed landscapes with geometric precision. But there was one thing he couldn't seem to be able to do: he could not get Grace Jackson to talk about herself.

Every question which he hoped would reveal a little bit about the woman sharing the bench seat of his pickup truck turned into a dissertation on her sister.

Have you ever been to Texas before?

The first word of her answer had been her sister's name. *Sophia's last movie was filmed just outside of Austin. We were here for almost three weeks of shooting last September. The flood damage was still really noticeable. I knew she'd agree to come this week for Texas Rescue because the destruction upset her at the time. I knew she'd like to help.*

His concern for Grace grew with every mile.

Last night, when all he'd been able to think about was this beautiful woman in his bed, he'd wanted to believe that he'd jumped to the wrong conclusions about her relationship with her sister. He'd heard a few manipulative comments, seen a few anxious hand gestures, but really, nothing extraordinary. Having just handled the Burns couple, he might have too easily assumed Sophia and Grace were in a dysfunctional relationship, as well.

Midnight was a convenient time to decide that he'd been wrong. If Grace wasn't really in trouble, then he could focus on her as a potential date—or to be brutally honest with himself, as a lover—rather than as someone who needed saving.

That had changed over pancakes. Listening to this morning's meeting with the publicist had been as sobering as a cold shower. Grace was clearly in a dysfunctional relationship with her sister. Still, he had been impressed with how she'd handled herself. She'd been outnumbered by the publicist and her sister. She didn't agree with their decisions and she'd seemed embarrassed by some of the discussion, but she'd handled herself with poise.

He would be able to help her this week. Grace wouldn't be one of those women who refused assistance. She wouldn't be like his mother, sticking with a family member who made her miserable for far too long. Grace was surely more like Mrs. Burns, ready to get out of a bad situation and move on with her life.

But that had been twenty-five miles ago. Twenty-five long miles during which only one subject had been covered: Sophia the Great.

"What did you study in college?" he asked, a direct question to Grace, about Grace.

"I didn't go to college. I was lucky to be able to work for Sophia right after high school. She had a scholarship to study theater at UCLA. She'd finished two years there when our parents died. She dropped out and came home just so I could finish high school in our hometown. She did a lot of local modeling and some local TV commercials. After that, we headed back to LA, but by then she felt the window of opportunity for her to get her degree had passed. Actresses need to work while they're young."

Incredible. Every single answer led back to Sophia.

He shouldn't be so surprised. Victims of domestic abuse could lose their own sense of self. He knew that, yet he'd truly thought Grace was more independent than this. She'd been assertive enough to come and find him in the ER's kitchen. She'd argued with hotel managers and publicists and him. Hell, she'd even had a face-to-face moment with an angry Mr. Burns. But now, she was all about Sophia, every second, every word. It was unhealthy.

He could see a traffic light ahead. It was time to make a judgment call. His plan had been to take her to his latest landscaping project, an outdoor space for a nursing home located in an Austin suburb. He'd thought she could decompress in a Zen-like contemplation of nature while he took some measurements and did some maintenance. After this nonstop Sophia-centric conversation, though, he wasn't sure that was a good idea. What would Grace think about, if he arranged time for her to have no other obligations? Sophia. That was the only thing on her mind.

Grace checked her cell phone. "She must not be awake yet. She hasn't texted me like I asked her to. Usually, she's really good about keeping in touch with people she cares about. She's not an inaccessible celebrity once you are part of her inner circle."

Weird. Just a weird thing to say. Was she trying to reassure herself that she was part of her own sister's inner circle?

Alex fell silent. Every attempt at conversation had been futile, anyway.

The silence didn't last long. "Where did you go to college?" Grace asked. It was the first question she'd initiated during the entire drive.

"Rice University for undergrad. Baylor for med school." He glanced over.

She was writing in her notebook. "When I type this up for Sophia, I could type up a list of identical facts for you. Baylor versus UCLA, that kind of thing. Sophia's really good at memorizing things that way, but I don't—"

"Grace." The traffic light up ahead turned yellow, then red. He stopped the truck gently when he wanted to slam on the brakes. "I know she has a good memory. You told me that. Three times."

"Oh." She scratched something out. "I won't type that in your notes, then."

His notes?

"Were all these Sophia stories supposed to be trivia I was memorizing about her?"

"Of course."

Jeez. Twenty-five miles of this. The conversation was still weird, but at least it made a little sense, in a Hollywood kind of way. If Grace had been writing things down, he would have realized what was going on sooner. He supposed she didn't take notes when she was the one doing the talking.

Her pencil was poised over her page now. "Our project this morning was to prepare you for the media scrutiny. Don't you feel like you know Sophia better now?"

"I've had more than enough of Sophia Jackson."

Grace's answering silence made him feel like a jerk. She was emotionally fragile. He should handle her with care.

Grace yanked open the tote bag at her feet and dropped

her notebook in it. It wasn't a very fragile move. "You're the one who kept asking me questions about her."

The light turned green. Alex turned in the opposite direction of the nursing home.

"I asked you about you," he said. "Where did *you* go to school? Where did *you* grow up?"

"I'm well aware that what people want to know is *where did the two of you grow up?* Why would anyone want to know those things about me?"

He pulled off the road and parked next to a building that was half gas station, half barbecue joint. It was early for lunch, but if they did the landscaping first, lunch would be late. He didn't want to risk Grace getting hypoglycemic again. She was in a delicate state already.

Grace kept staring straight ahead, even after he killed the engine. She didn't look delicate; she looked angry. He'd been afraid that she was obsessed with her sister, but now he suspected she was obsessed with her job. That seemed marginally more normal, but it still indicated that she lacked balance in her life.

He strove for balance in his. He made sure his emotions were in check before he spoke. "I didn't realize we were cramming for an exam about your sister's life. The last half hour would have made more sense, then."

She sighed in defeat. "It's okay. I'll put everything I told you in writing."

"Don't. You have enough work to do. I may not have memorized a new scene after having the screenwriter read it out loud to me once, just once, while I was having my hair and makeup done on site in a remote part of Tunisia, before running to a hilltop and nailing the scene in one take, getting every word right and catching the light as the sun rose, thus saving the cast and crew and production company from having to strike the set and repeat the entire process the next day at great cost, but I do have a decent memory."

She stared at him, mouth open in surprise. He gently used one finger under her chin to close it, smiling to soften his sarcasm. "Don't be so shocked. Doctors have to memorize a lot of stuff, too. I'm officially declaring a lunch break. No notebooks, no phones. Just brisket."

Grace frowned down at the phone in her hand. "I think we should have a working lunch. We don't have a lot of time."

"We have a week until this ball. Sophia is living in my house. I'm going to get to know her whether I want to or not."

Grace looked at him then, her special blend of hope and worry in her eyes. "But you do want to get to know her, don't you?"

That made him pause. "This is supposed to be about photos. What's really going on here?"

"You're supposed to be her boyfriend. You're supposed to be the reason she's no longer interested in Deezee. We're establishing a better life for her."

"You can't establish a better life for someone. They have to choose it. As for the boyfriend thing, the term was *fake* boyfriend, if my memory serves—which I'm certain it does. However, since I'm not an actor, I'm not going to try to fake that I like her. It's fortunate that I don't need to fake anything."

"Oh, good."

She said it with such relief, it silenced him. Did she want him to be her sister's real boyfriend?

"You and Sophia are perfect for one another."

When a goat eats a wolf.

Grace had to feel the chemistry toward him that he felt toward her. He hadn't imagined those fingertips trailing along his waist last night. Her arousal had been revealed by her clinging white pajamas and her quickened breaths. How could she want him to want someone else instead?

"Let me be clear. I mean that I don't need to fake anything in order to pull off a photo op at this ball. I'm not going to fake that I have more of a relationship with Sophia than I do. I'm not going to worry about who is a reporter and who isn't, because I'm only going to tell the truth. I met her when she came into the emergency room with a suspected fracture. I offered her a place to stay because she couldn't make her flight. Because I'm bringing her to the ball as my date, good manners and common courtesy require me to do my best to make sure she has a pleasant evening. We'll sit together for dinner, we'll dance if her ankle allows, we'll talk. If the public wants to jump to conclusions, that's not in my control."

"Martina will control it. She'll make sure everyone jumps to conclusions. She'll imply you knew each other before the ER visit. So will Sophia." Grace turned those beautiful brown-gold eyes away from him. "So will I."

"Is that what you want?" He touched her again, his fingertips light against her jaw as he turned her face toward him.

She kept her eyes downcast. "It's my job."

"I don't have to do any of this," he said. "Neither do you."

He had a long moment to study the feathering of her lashes, dark against her skin, until she opened her eyes and looked at him, startlingly direct. "You said you would. You're supposed to be a man of your word." She jerked her chin free.

Rejection. Abandonment. He let go of her instantly. If she didn't want him, then he didn't want her, either.

A part of him knew that wasn't true. The angry self-defense was an old reflex, born from the need to protect himself from all the miseries of a violent parent. *I don't care about you, either, Papa.*

He'd spent his adult life mastering that negative emotion. He didn't have to react defensively to Grace's rejection, but control required consciousness. Introspection. Focus.

They were on their way to build a garden to give other people a place to focus their thoughts, but right now, with the feel of Grace's skin still fresh on his fingertips, he was having a hard time keeping his own wants and needs straight. Rejection had a way of screwing with a man's mind.

He got out of the truck and shoved the key in the front pocket of his jeans. The feel of the packed dirt under his work boots and the smell of the barbecue's wood smoke centered him. He walked around the front of the truck and opened Grace's door with equanimity.

Because he was calm, he could see that she was not. She'd put her tote bag in her lap, and her knuckles were white as she clenched the handles in her fists. He noticed the tension in the way she held her neck and remembered his desire yesterday to smooth his hands over her shoulders to release all that tightness. That desire was stronger, now that he knew her better. The truth was, he wanted Grace, even if she did not want him.

"I'm sorry," she said, not quite meeting his eyes. "I shouldn't have said that about keeping your word. You've done so much for us, and I keep asking you to do more."

It didn't matter what her job was or who she was related to. It didn't even matter that he knew in advance she'd disappear from his life. Something inside him responded to everything about her. He wanted to be her lover, but she needed a friend—and he wanted to be what she needed.

"I offered you a place to stay. I offered to take your sister to the ball. You'd don't need to say 'I'm sorry' just because you said yes."

He offered her his hand. She pushed the tote bag onto the seat and took his hand, then jumped gracefully from the high cab to the ground. Neither of them let go.

Be her friend. She needs a friend.

Standing a little too close to her, their hands linked by their thighs, he spoke quietly. "Everything I offered was to help you, Grace Jackson. I'm giving you my word that I'm on your side. You said this morning you thought Sophia should tell the truth. You thought Sophia should go to the ball alone. If you still want to go that route, I'll back you up."

"Thank you." She sounded breathless. She sounded like she had at midnight.

He wanted to kiss her. He did not.

"But she's not just my sister, she's my boss. She usually has good instincts. I think I should do my job."

"Then I'll support you on that, too."

"Which means you'll take her to the ball." But her gaze had dropped to his mouth

"Of course." He waited, every muscle aching to reach for her, the woman who needed a friend.

She still didn't let go of his hand, but with a sigh that sounded like defeat, Grace reached up to the bench seat with her other hand to grab her tote bag.

He stopped her by placing his hand over hers. "Sometimes a job is nothing but a job. Why don't you leave that here? I meant what I said about taking a lunch break. No work."

They stood in the shelter of the truck's open door, each with an arm resting on the seat, hands touching, their bodies open to one another, only inches of air keeping her chest from his. He took a deliberate, calm breath. This wasn't the time to give in to that physical awareness.

Under his palm, Grace's hand formed a fist around the bag's strap. "We could work on your project over lunch instead. Plan our schedules for the week, for the times we'll be...together."

"Leave it." *And don't look at me like that.*

That inch of air between them was full of heat and electricity.

She let her gaze drop to his chest, then lower, the same as she had at midnight. Any sane man would move away at this moment, but the torture was too addictive.

She's leaving at the end of the week. The truth of that should kill his desire.

It didn't. He watched her breasts rise as she took her own deep breath before she let go of the bag's strap, her fingers uncurling under his hand.

"Then what will we talk about?" she asked.

"We'll get to know one another, like any man and woman do. There's nothing to memorize. We can say anything."

"I don't think I've been in that position before. Not since I was a teenager."

He saw her mouth form the words, but he barely heard them over the hum of arousal in his brain. His own voice was low. "You and I aren't famous. No one will care what happens between us. Except us."

And then there was no air between them. Bodies touched, shirt brushing blouse, mouth on soft mouth. The kiss they should have had at midnight was too intense at noon, but they were swept into it together, mouths open and tasting and taking. When she made a little sound of greed, he let go of her hands and pulled her into his arms, a feeling of *yes, this* and *finally* as he molded her pliant body to his.

When her hand slid up his back pocket to cling to his leather belt, when her fingers dug into the hair at the nape of his neck, the sound of greed came from him. They made love with their mouths, hot and moist. Intimate. Jeans became the worst possible piece of clothing. His were tight and restrictive, hers were a coarse barrier to the soft curves he wanted to feel, and—

And there was nothing he could do about it. They were in a parking lot, about to be surrounded by a lunch crowd.

It didn't matter. He didn't want to give up any taste of Grace he could have.

The frustration was exquisite, but it was building too hot, too fast, so he forced himself to end the kiss. Kissed her once more. Ended that, but didn't move away from her. After a moment of listening to her pant for breath, he kissed the soft skin of her cheek, but his control was a flimsy thing. He needed to put space between them. He placed his palm on the metal of the truck, breathed in Grace one more time, and pushed himself away.

"Wow," she whispered.

He nodded, trying not to think, not to feel.

A work truck parked beside them. Grace moved out of the way, so Alex could shut his truck door and let the other driver open his. He kept his back to Grace, standing between her and the driver. He didn't want another man seeing her sexy, just-kissed look. Behind him, he heard Grace's breathy, bedroom voice.

"Wow," she repeated. "That was a huge mistake."

Chapter Fifteen

Grace knew she was a good personal assistant. She never missed a detail or dropped an assignment. She knew how to handle celebrities. She could hold her own against a publicist. But there was one thing she couldn't do: she couldn't make Alex Gregory tell a lie.

So she skipped that part.

"I won't ask you to lie, but could you at least not mention that you kissed her sister?" That didn't sound fair. It wasn't as if the kiss had been all one-sided. "Or that her sister kissed you?"

"You don't need anyone's permission to kiss anyone you want."

"I know that." She kept her eyes on the picnic table. A huge chunk of beef brisket sat on white butcher paper, looking like a pot roast for the two of them to share, along with breaded and fried jalapeño peppers and two plastic bowls of banana pudding. It might be typically Texan, but it was the strangest array of food she'd ever seen at a lunch, working or not. It added to her feeling of disorientation.

She should be consulting stylists and lining up fittings for her sister, or making lists of local press and arranging transportation. Instead, she was eating at a table outside of a restaurant that had gas pumps, as if the cars and trucks needed to be fed, too, while she sat across from a man that she so desperately, physically craved. She didn't want to eat. All she wanted to do was plaster herself against his shockingly strong, deliciously warm body and kiss him until her brain dissolved. That way, she wouldn't have to think about the mess she'd just created.

Her hands were tempted to reach over the table to brush his hair back from his forehead. She interlocked her fingers tightly, just to sit still. "We're supposed to be making you into the perfect man for her. I don't think the perfect boyfriend would kiss her sister."

"Fake boyfriend. For one date."

"I know that." She clenched her hands tighter. If she'd been holding a pencil, it would have snapped by now.

"For what it's worth, I have no intention of telling Sophia I kissed you when we get back to the house."

She winced and leaned forward to whisper. "Don't use her name outside of your house, okay?"

He shook his head slowly. There was no mistaking that sad downturn to his kissable mouth, that wrinkle of worry on his brow. He pitied her.

"I'm not being paranoid," she said.

"I mean this as kindly as possible, but yes, you are being paranoid. Look around you. This isn't LA. This isn't even Austin."

Obediently, Grace looked to the nearest patron, who sat at least six feet away at another picnic table. He was tearing the meat off some ribs with his teeth, elbows on the table, ball cap on his head. He said something to his table partner, a similarly attired man, as he chewed. All Grace could pick out from their conversation were a few numbers. She looked back to Alex.

"They're talking about tractor tires," he said.

"It's still a good habit to get into, not saying names. You'll need that this week."

"I'm not going to tell *her* about kissing you because it's none of her business. I absolutely have no obligation to report to her what I was doing and with whom I was doing it. I'm very sorry that you think you do."

Did she? Grace hadn't really thought it through, this instinctive need for secrecy. "It's not like I have to tell her, but…"

She fell silent. Did it matter now if her sister found out Grace had a thing for Alex?

The damage was done.

She'd had a whole week, a golden opportunity to give her sister the experience of being with a man who didn't treat her like she was lucky to get his time. A chance to remind Sophia that there were men out there who liked women as people, not as accessories. A chance for Sophia to live in a real house and be treated like a real person instead of a celebrity. A chance to take care of Sophia in return for the years she'd taken care of Grace. One week—and Grace had ruined her big chance to change her sister's life on the first day.

As she stared into Alex's sky-blue eyes and struggled for something to say, it hit her: she wouldn't have missed that kiss for the world. Not even for the sister who'd been her world. Having been held and kissed and wanted by Alex, there was no way she could possibly encourage Alex to hold and kiss and want anyone else.

What kind of sister am I?

Grace put her hands over her face, and tried not to cry.

* * *

Alex should have seen this coming. For a doctor who'd treated dozens of victims of domestic violence, for a son who'd lived through his mother's multiple attempts to leave his abusive father, he should have known it would be hard on Grace to do anything independently of her sister. *You knew she needed a friend, not a lover. You couldn't just be content being her friend, though, could you?*

He rounded the edge of the table to go to Grace's side. The men at the next table had noticed that a pretty woman was sniffing back tears and hiding her face, of course, and they were doing their best not to stare. Alex straddled the plank seat, facing Grace and keeping his back to the men to give her some illusion of privacy.

Their kiss had triggered these tears, somehow. He remembered the kitchen at midnight, the way she'd whispered *I can't*. He hesitated now to hold her again. Falling back on his experience as a doctor, he tried to maintain a caring objectivity. He reached for the roll of paper towels on the table and tore off a sheet and held it out to her, but with her hands hiding her face, she didn't see it.

"Grace," he said, feeling like a physician, "it's going to be okay."

She burst into tears in earnest.

To hell with it. He pulled her closer, so her body was in the V of his legs, and wrapped one arm around her to anchor her to him. With his hand, he pressed her tearful face into his shoulder.

"I don't want you to be scared of Sophia."

"I'm not scared of Sophia."

"Then what are you scared of? What terrible thing will happen if she finds out we like one another?"

"I...never mind. I can't explain. It's so embarrassing."

She pressed her forehead into his shoulder, hiding. He

remembered seeing his mother looking into the mirror, the bruise on her cheek darkening by the moment. The way she'd spotted him and covered her cheek with her hand and turned her face away, embarrassed. *Oh, my little bear. I can't explain anything right now. You don't worry about Mama, okay?*

He'd never asked his mother to explain it, not even when he was a teenager and it was just the two of them, learning a new life in the land of cowboys and cattle. They'd once been so close. Even as a very young child, he'd witnessed everything she did to expose the dangerous factory. Then later, he'd been old enough to help hide money, hide identification cards, hide food. They'd survived together, then eventually thrived together. They should be close now, or close still, but there was a wall between them, built of the things they did not discuss.

Walls were too sturdy. He didn't want to begin building one here, with this woman. He laid his cheek against her hair. "Can you explain to me why that kiss was a mistake?"

"First, you have to promise not to laugh at me for being stupid."

"I promise." What an easy promise to make. He'd just shared the best kiss of his life with a woman who was crying. He'd never felt further from laughing.

"The thing is…" She lifted her head enough to peek around them to ensure that the other outdoor diners were still at distant tables. "I'm afraid Deezee will try to win her back at some point. It's possible Martina will advise him to. I thought if you and my sister were into each other, then she might not fall back into Deezee's trap. You're nice to her. You bring her ice and pancakes and you covered her with a blanket. You can't imagine how long it's been since she's had someone other than me be nice to her. I wanted her to be with a good man, but now I've stolen you away."

It was a good thing she couldn't see his face, because he had to smile into her hair, a little moment of pleasure. She'd stolen him, had she?

"You didn't deprive your sister of anything."

"I disagree. I think you're something very special."

The pleasure, so mixed with the pain...

Her tears were very real. She carried a terrible guilt. It was as if she didn't think she had a right to anything she wanted or needed. Only Sophia's needs mattered.

"I meant that your sister didn't lose out on a relationship with me, because she never had a chance. It's been you from the moment I first laid eyes on you."

Grace went very still in his arms.

He was being too intense, talking like a lover. She needed a friend.

He let go of her and sat back a few inches. With the paper towel, he dried the cheek he'd so recently kissed in the parking lot. "When I walked through that curtain and first saw you, I must have looked like an idiot. You knocked the words right out of my head. I just stared at you."

"I thought you were disappointed in me. You said, 'You're the assistant?' like you couldn't believe it."

"I was expecting someone like Martina. I saw an angel The only reason I agreed to take Sophia to the ball was so that you wouldn't spend this week helping some other man get ready. I wanted you to myself. Pretty devious of me, if you think about it."

He smiled at her; tears welled in her eyes.

"I'm no angel. I'm a terrible sister. Do you remember when I said I couldn't stand by and watch Sophia crash? I didn't tell you the whole truth. I'd decided this week would be her last chance." She waved those words away quickly with her hand, and started over. "I mean, this week was *my* last chance to see if I could save her from herself. And if I couldn't, if she continued to follow Deezee's lead in everything, I was ready to move out."

Words spoken on that metal bench burst from his memory. *I'm the one that's getting sick of it.* If she'd already decided to leave, then he wouldn't have to help her make those decisions. He wouldn't have to wait while she worked through those issues. The physical desire he'd been trying to tame roared back to life. Friends could become lovers. They could take that kiss as far as they wanted it to go.

"I've got a list." She fiercely dashed her cheek on her sleeve. "It's in my tote bag. Just some different options and th-things I'd have to take care of if I decided to move out on my own."

Yeah, he was a hell of a friend, all right. His mind was skipping ahead to taking her to bed, to losing himself in all the shades of gold that made up Grace Jackson, while she was worrying about her future. He handed her the paper towel and eased himself back a little farther.

She mopped up the last of her own tears. "But Deezee made that decision for Sophia, didn't he? He left her high and dry, so I guess that's that. I'm staying now."

To his surprise, she plunged her hands through her own hair, squeezing her skull. "Why am I not happy about this?"

Because you don't really want to go back to the way things were.

"I'm glad Deezee's gone," she said. "But Sophia didn't make any decisions. I wanted her to choose."

Alex stayed quiet and listened, feeling humbled. He'd thought he'd be the one to lead Grace to all these revelations this week. He was so accustomed as an emergency physician to being the one who stated the problem out loud and offered the solution. *I don't think you fell down a staircase. There is legal and financial help available today. You don't have to leave with the man who hurt you.*

But Grace was not a patient. She was already aware and ready to change her life. Listening to her was a revelation. Some victims found their own way out. He knew that; he just never witnessed it. He only saw the women in his ER who were still trapped.

My mother got out.

Another revelation. He'd never thought of it that way. Officially, they'd escaped from the political corruption that had followed the collapse of the Soviet government. His mother had exposed the factory conditions, putting a political target on her back—for which his father had shaken her, the back of her head smacking into a picture frame, shattering the glass, the blood matting her hair. *How could you bring this down on us?*

It was the first time his father had hurt his mother. She'd later been jailed by the people his father had been trying to curry favor with. *I was going to be made a Party member. You've ruined my life.*

She'd dared to seek asylum in a foreign land, but Alex realized now she'd escaped from an abusive husband at the same time. Papa had stayed on shore as their unauthorized boat had ventured into deep waters. They'd sailed from Russia to Turkey, their identities a life-or-death secret. Then they'd walked from embassy to embassy, using their real names, hoping his mother's reputation as an engineer would be their saving grace. It had been. They'd been flown to Houston, Texas, where she could teach at Rice University. His mother had been victorious.

Why was it more comfortable to remember her as a victim?

"I wanted Sophie to decide if she still wanted her career and everything that goes with it. There's a lot of sacrifice involved. She can't even go to a grocery store. I thought maybe she was done with it all, and that was why she was self-destructing." Grace let her hands fall into her lap. "I'll never know now. Sophie will make this Texas Rescue appearance a triumph. She wants Deezee to regret what he's done, and she'll do that by being more successful than ever."

"Good for Sophie. What about Grace? What will you do after this week?"

"I guess we keep going, the same as we have for years."

Selfishly, he wanted her to let Sophia return to LA without her. A week would not be enough time with Grace. He slid the butcher paper closer and pulled two battered metal forks out of a tin pail that held table settings, buying himself time to be sure he would speak from a neutral position, as a friend.

He handed her a fork. "Deezee didn't take away your options. If anything on your list is more appealing to you than continuing on that same path, then it doesn't matter what Deezee does. You get to choose your own path."

"I hadn't thought of it like that." She bit her lower lip, as she had yesterday.

He only had to bend his head, and her lips would be soft beneath his. He so badly wanted to kiss her. He held himself still.

Customers had begun spilling out of the indoor area, taking up more picnic tables as the lunch hour reached its peak. Grace slid a quick glance at each new table, calculating how freely she could speak. It was one of those sacrifices that went with the American obsession with fame, one he'd never taken seriously before. He did now.

"I can take you somewhere quiet," he began, but the rest of his thought about his volunteer project was completely swamped by the image of taking Grace somewhere quiet, just the two of them. If they had privacy, they wouldn't use it to think.

He was surely reading too much into her expression, a little surprised, a little…hopeful? She lowered her gaze, waiting for the rest of his invitation, and damn it, he wanted to kiss her again.

The last kiss had left her weeping.

He grabbed his fork and returned to the other side of the table, taking himself firmly into the friend zone, where she needed him to be. "I'm redoing a meditation garden at a nursing home. That's my project. I've got some repairs to make on a wall."

Two men sat heavily at the other end of their picnic table. He exchanged a courtesy nod with them. Strangers shared the long tables at places like this. Paper towels, utensils and condiments were all in the middle for anyone to grab.

Grace sat up a little straighter. "You make gardens for nursing homes?"

She might have been turning the conversation to something less personal for her, but it stayed personal for him. The gardens were his private outlet. "Nursing homes, rehab facilities. Wherever I happen to hear someone has the space for me to build something."

"Is this garden going to be like your backyard? I think that look is really beautiful."

Ah, the pleasure of a sincere compliment. "I'm glad you like it. This project has a long way to go, but it would give you some uninterrupted time to think about what you want. Anything you want."

One of the men at their table reached for a squeeze bottle of barbecue sauce, and Grace pushed it his way without waiting for him to ask. That was Grace. Always on high alert, always looking to make things easier for everyone else.

"That sounds nice," she said, "but we're supposed to be working together."

"I'm just going to pick up a load of gravel and deliver it to the site. Letting you have a chance to unwind after the stress you've been through is the least I can do."

She seemed to be back in control of herself, and he didn't want to upset her equilibrium again. He chose his words with care. "I'm sorry I added to that stress. I won't make the same mistake twice. Anything you don't want to happen, won't happen."

He raised his cup of banana pudding to her as if he were proposing a toast. "Eat up. We need to go buy some rocks."

I won't make the same mistake twice.

Grace had the peaceful surroundings of a rock garden under construction in which to stew over that particular statement. She was the one who'd said that incredible kiss was a mistake, and now Alex was sorry for it. She'd never had a man apologize for kissing her.

It sucked.

She wanted to make that same mistake again. She was supposed to be contemplating her future, but all she could contemplate was Alex's body. Under that faded red T-shirt, there were serious muscles at work as he hauled wheelbarrows full of gravel to bare spots in the garden. With a shovel first, and then a rake, he smoothed everything into place around the pillars of cypress trees. From her little perch on top of a limestone wall, she watched.

She was terrible at meditation. The only thing she seemed to be able to contemplate was how much warmer it would have to get before Alex would remove his shirt. The sun was plenty warm on her shoulders, and she wasn't doing anything physical like he was. More than once, he'd grabbed the bottom edge of his shirt as if he were going to pull it off over his head.

Yes, please.

But he'd glanced her way, and left the shirt on.

She gave up on meditation and opened her notebook, ready to brainstorm her options and then make a list of pros and cons for each possible choice. Instead, she drew little squiggly shapes in the margins, and turned his words over in her mind. *Anything you don't want to happen, won't happen.* What about the things she did want to happen? If she wanted another kiss that drove every thought out of her mind, was he up for that?

Apparently not. She couldn't be too shocked if a boy wasn't turned on by a girl who cried hard enough to soak a paper towel after being kissed. No wonder he was giving her space.

Alex tossed the shovel and rake into the empty wheelbarrow, then lifted the edge of his shirt high, using the bottom hem to wipe his forehead. His bare torso was tan all over, as if he usually worked without a shirt, and every muscle in his chest and abs was defined. The man had to be zero-percent body fat.

Let's make another mistake. Heck, let's screw up everything completely.

He dropped his shirt back in place, picked up the handles of his empty wheelbarrow, and headed for the truck that was parked off to her left. She heard the scrape of the shovel and the tumbling of rocks into the wheelbarrow. In an effort to look busy herself, she flipped from her *Options* page to the list Sophia had dictated earlier. *Spray tan* got a black line through it. So did *personal trainer.*

She closed her notebook and went back to contemplating the beauty of nature—if a man's sculpted body counted as a natural wonder.

If the man was Alex Gregory, it did.

Chapter Sixteen

Alex had to work at the ER the next few days. The routine allowed them to settle into a sort of domestic tranquility.

He'd come home from the hospital, endure some sweet torture in the close proximity of the kitchen as he helped Grace finish cooking whatever she'd decided to experiment with that day for dinner, and then the three of them would crash in the living room. Grace would stay busy on her laptop, assuring him she wasn't working. Her sister was usually on her phone, but when she put a movie on, as she did every evening, Alex noticed she gave it her full attention. Her occasional commentary was usually snarky, and usually directed at something he hadn't even noticed, like a change in a scene's lighting. He sat in the armchair, flipping through medical journals, and tried not to be too obvious as he admired Grace's bare legs as she curled up in a corner of his couch wearing khaki shorts. Between those bare legs and the memory of the taste of her mouth...

He stretched out on that couch every night and waited, eyes well-adjusted to the dark, for the sight of Grace slipping into the kitchen for a midnight glass of milk. Every night, he was disappointed.

But every day, he saw signs that made him glad he'd opened his house to Grace Jackson. Despite the fact that Deezee was no longer in the picture, there were no indications that Sophia was becoming the paragon of a sister that Grace claimed she'd once been, but he could definitely see that Grace was done waiting for that miracle transformation.

His own surface transformation was nearly complete. Grace had arranged for an optical technician to bring designer frames and a large mirror into the ER's kitchen, and new frames for his existing prescription had been ordered with astounding ease. The hair stylist had arrived at his home one evening, all scissors and sass with a Malibu tan. She'd flown in from California for other South-by celebrities and would be returning the day of the ball to make up Sophia. She'd left his hair on the long side, cutting and trimming infinitesimal amounts of hair until every time she asked him to shake his head, his hair would fall into place to her satisfaction.

The end result had drawn an alarming amount of attention to him at work today. As far as he could tell, his brown frames had been replaced by black ones that were, granted, a little more sleek and touched with silver on the edges, and his hair had gone from being unintentionally shaggy to deliberately tousled, but neither change had been very significant. An absurd quantity of women at West Central Texas Hospital seemed to disagree. His eyes were suddenly a noticeable shade of blue. His hair had to be admired from every angle. It had been a relief to come home to the quiet of Grace and her sister.

He flipped the pages of his medical journal to a new study on blood thinners. Sophia turned off the movie she'd started twenty minutes earlier, but stayed languidly draped over the couch. "I can't believe that excuse for a film made it onto a single screen. Get me my tablet, Grace."

Grace stopped typing on her laptop instantly, but she didn't jump to do her sister's bidding as she had over pancakes on that first morning. "You know, you could ask that a little more nicely."

Alex looked up from his magazine.

"Get my tablet, *please*." The way Sophia drew out the word *please* was plainly obnoxious.

"No, thank you," Grace said with equally insincere politeness.

"What?"

Alex turned the page, although he hadn't read a word.

"If you want your tablet, it's charging in the bedroom, in the same place I've been putting it all week."

"You have to get it for me." Sophia jerked herself a little more upright. "I'm in a *cast*."

"It's a walking boot. You're supposed to be walking in it."

"I can't."

Alex turned another page, and tried to sound more bored than amused. "And yet, you must have made it to the kitchen today to get yourself a sandwich while we were scouting out the venue for the ball. You left the mayonnaise on the counter."

He hid a smile at Princess Picasso's go-to-hell look.

"Which reminds me," Sophia said to Grace, not deigning to respond to Alex, "have the grocery service send in that ancient-grain bread. I had to use mayonnaise today because there isn't any gochujang here." She snapped her fingers. "Oh—we need ube chips."

Grace shut the lid on her laptop and left, heading for the guest bedroom. Sophia shot him a look of triumph when Grace returned with the tablet, but as she held up one hand regally to receive it, Grace started tapping its screen.

"Stop that." Sophia lifted her head. Frowned. Pushed herself up to a sitting position. "Are you getting into my stuff? How are you getting into my stuff?"

"Deezee's birthday. Why is that still your password?"

"Give it here. What are you doing?"

"I'm giving you something to think about besides purple yam chips. I'm side-loading a script you were supposed to have read two weeks ago. They expected to hear from you yesterday. It's a very hot property, and your time is running out before they offer it to someone else."

"Whatever."

"It's Quentin. That Quentin."

Alex raised an eyebrow. The director's movies were critical successes, box office smashes—and famously violent.

"Great." Sophia made it sound like it was anything but. "They probably want me to go down in a blaze of gunfire."

"If they do, you can bank on it being very well choreographed, very big box office, very *Quentin* gunfire," Grace said.

Sophia pouted. "It's like my specialty now. I die in all these movies. Kill off the Jackson character, so we can watch her die in close-up. It's so stupid."

Grace stopped in mid-swipe. "You used to say it was storytelling. Do you want to read this?"

Sophia yawned. Alex knew her well enough now to suspect that she might have faked that perfectly timed yawn. It was hard to tell with an actress.

"I don't feel like it right now," Sophia said. "Maybe next week."

"Not giving them an answer is an answer."

Sophia didn't answer.

Alex watched, waiting, ready to help Grace in any way.

Grace held up the tablet, deadly serious. "This is it, then. You've come to a point in your life where you want to turn down a script from one of the directors you've dreamed of working with, without reading it or explaining why. You have that option, but be certain it's what you want. You can't rebound from this by posting a few clever quips on social media or finding a handsome man with blue eyes to help you save your pride. Make sure you're ready for your life to go in a different direction."

Silence stretched. Alex had been ready to rescue Grace for nearly a week, ever since the moment he'd seen her anxiety in the emergency room. He should have realized Grace could save herself.

"Give me my tablet." Sophia held up her hand, every bit as firm in her expression as Grace.

Grace gave it to her. At the tap of Sophia's finger, the recognizable color scheme of a social media site appeared. She settled back into her languid, lazy position, rocking her booted foot slowly from side to side.

Grace bowed her head, but Alex didn't think it was in defeat. She was only acknowledging the decision made. He felt the gravity of the moment, the end of a career, the wasting of a talent.

"I'm going to get some ice water," Grace said. She hadn't gone three steps toward the kitchen when Sophia stopped her with a tone of voice that Alex hadn't heard her use before.

"Gracie?" She sounded a little panicky. "Did you delete that script? I can't find it."

Grace froze, her back to her sister. "It's under the e-reader function."

"I don't know what *side-loading* means. I only know the social media apps." The sound of Sophia swallowing her pride was practically audible. "Would you please show me?"

Alex understood Grace's look of relief. She'd finally forced Sophia to make a choice, and Sophia had made the smart choice. Their lives would keep going as they were. Alex had to agree that was a better option than self-destructing for the love of the unfaithful boyfriend, but their lives would take them right back to LA.

He stared at the medical journal, open now to the wrong page.

I knew Grace would disappear. I knew which day she'd go. I kissed her only once. Once cannot change my life.

Sophia planted her boot on the ground and stood up. "I'll bring it to you. I'm thirsty, too." She thumped across his polished concrete floor, put her arm around Grace and disappeared into his kitchen, taking away the woman who no longer needed him to save her.

Alex got up, too, and went outside. In the dark, the inanimate rocks that made up his garden were precisely as he'd arranged them. Next week, when Grace and her sister were back in LA, he would take some satisfaction in imagining the women living well, just as he imagined for the patients he helped for a brief time in his emergency room.

I'd go crazy wondering how everyone is. How do you handle the not knowing?

He'd have more than his imagination in this case, actually. He'd be able to see Sophia's success, and he'd know for certain that Grace was doing well then, too. It would be more than he ever had with his patients, closer to what he had with his mother. He didn't have to imagine that his mother was doing well. He knew for certain she was chairing the university's engineering department and traveling on her personal quest for better education around the world.

His mother, his emergency patients and Grace Jackson. He helped them, then they left. He wished them well.

He put his foot on a low limestone wall, so like the one he and Grace had worked on at the nursing home this week. When Grace left, he'd carry on exactly as he had before he'd ever seen her brown-gold eyes looking at him like she hoped he could save her. His well-balanced life would be unchanged. This week had not derailed his life.

Perhaps nothing could.

He shoved at the wall with his foot, a sudden burst of frustration that accomplished nothing. The wall did not budge. What had he expected? The pattern was set.

I could change it.

To what? He had no other pattern to follow. He helped people in need, and then he moved on. Next patient. Next garden.

But there'd never be another Grace.

It was only one kiss.

He kicked the wall once more, and headed back into the house.

Alex knew Grace needed his help with one last thing: the Black and White Ball.

More accurately, her sister needed his help, but Grace and her sister were inextricably linked. What helped Sophia, helped Grace. And so, on one of the last days Alex would have Grace in his life, his house was invaded by a team of stylists and seamstresses.

They rearranged his furniture and brought in entire clothing racks of evening gowns and tuxedos, all carefully wrapped in plain cloth bags in case there were paparazzi hiding in his bushes, trying to get a scoop on what Sophia Jackson might wear to this gala. The secrecy wasn't necessary. No one had thought to look for a movie star in the home of an ER doctor, and surely no one would care whether that doctor wore Armani or Tom Ford or Calvin Klein.

These people cared, though. It could not possibly matter in the grand scheme of life whether his pockets were slit or had flaps, whether his coat had one button or two, whether the satin of the lapel would reflect well in photographs. It could not matter, but the stylists were deadly serious about every detail, Sophia almost as committed. Grace, ever supportive of her sister, offered thoughtful opinions.

She'd done the same for him, this week in the garden. Did it really matter if he trimmed back an overgrown peach tree by two feet or three? And yet, Grace had stood patiently on the ground, pointing out each branch that needed to be evened up, so that he didn't have to keep climbing down to judge for himself.

His sense of fairness demanded that he treat this project with the same respect. When they asked for his opinion, he gave it: he'd wear the Armani.

Once that was decided, he was expected to stay and give an opinion on the gowns. On colors and hems and accessories— good God. It was beyond frivolous.

Sophia was spending her first day out of the boot, adjusting to the ankle wrap. She didn't want to put her ankle through the standing and sitting and stepping in and out of multiple gowns. Grace was acting as her double. To him, the sisters were so different, with Grace's warm gold so much more appealing than her sister's platinum, that he hadn't realized they were nearly the same build and exactly the same height.

With Grace as the model, the succession of gowns became an excuse to openly admire the woman he should have kissed a thousand times this week.

Too late.

The only purpose he served was to stand by in his tuxedo. He wasn't treating illness and injury. He wasn't clearing a garden path so a wheelchair could fit easily. He wasn't even reading clinical studies on trauma methodology. Instead, when a gown received general approval from the team, he stood next to Grace so everyone could evaluate how their clothing would photograph together.

"Now put your arm around her. Hmm... I see the problem, the skirt gets pushed off center if she gets close to him." The stylist walked to the other side of the room. "Especially noticeable from this angle. Grace, move a little bit to your left."

Sophia scrutinized them. "But I'm going to need to stand very close to him. Put your arm around his waist, Grace. Let me see what that does to the silhouette of the gown."

The feast for his eyes became a feast for his senses every time he touched Grace. The scent of her each time she cuddled into his side was like rain in the desert that had been his week in the friend zone. Every gown left her shoulders and arms bare, and the feel of her skin whetted his appetite for more.

More what? A one-night stand with a woman you know will disappear the next day?

It would be a novel twist in the pattern of his life, at least.

The next gown had plenty of *more*. The skirt was full and fit for a princess, but the plunging neckline was scandalous, revealing Grace's body all the way to her navel. The V was too wide just as it was too deep. Instead of revealing her cleavage, the dress exposed the full curve of each perfect breast, modesty only barely maintained by the fabric strapping that covered the center of each breast.

Alex said nothing. He could hardly think straight. Mere mortals didn't wear gowns like that in the real world. She looked like a movie star.

He was aware, suddenly, that Grace was looking right at him, her unique blend of worry and hope bright in her eyes. What reaction was she looking for?

"That's the one," Sophia declared.

Alex bit out the phrase the stylist had been using all morning to dismiss Grace from the room. "You can change now."

Sophia laughed. "No, she can't. I want to take a picture of you two together first. I need to see how this one photographs."

"You're not wearing that tomorrow, Sophia."

"Oh, yes I am. Every man who sees me will have the same reaction as you. You can't take your eyes off her."

He tore his gaze from Grace and rounded on her sister. "If you wear that, the deal is off. This is real life. My real life. I'm not going to introduce you to my coworkers and have them not know where to look while they're trying to eat a damned dinner with their wives."

"This is about making a statement. And that dress makes exactly the statement I want to make."

Alex knew what message that dress sent to men, because he was hearing it loud and clear. Grace looked deliberately provocative, yet she looked like a woman who was all the more powerful because she could send men's thoughts in the direction she chose—as if he needed to be provoked to want to take Grace to bed.

He gritted his teeth. "Not tomorrow. That dress says—"

"It says Oscars," Grace interrupted. "Maybe even Met

Gala. But for this week, it's too much, Sophie. You're re-establishing your reputation as a smart, mature—"

"Would you quit using that word? Yo, Alex." Sophia bumped him with her shoulder. "Stop drooling on the Armani. That's my baby sister you're staring at."

The stylist thrust a metallic silver gown between them. "I was saving the best for last, but maybe we should try it on now."

Alex and Sophia waited in frosty silence.

Grace returned to the living room in a column of silver. It covered her from a simple circle at the base of her throat to the tips of her polished toes, skimming over her body without clinging. There was something innocent about it—short sleeves, Alex realized, almost a schoolgirl look. Although the sleeves and the neckline appeared demure at first glance, they were made of silver netting that allowed the warmth of her skin to show through. She didn't look like a sexual fantasy and she didn't look like an untouchable movie star. She looked like an incredibly lovely Grace Jackson.

"That's the one," Alex said. When he felt Sophia's stare, he realized he'd said it almost reverently. He ignored Sophia.

"Isn't it perfect?" the stylist asked. "An echo of that Audrey Hepburn spirit we captured during last year's award season, but the column dress says modern and smart."

Alex didn't wait for a request to stand next to Grace. He walked up to her, tuning out the cluster of people who'd invaded his house. "You look very, very beautiful."

"Thank you."

Princess Picasso gave an order. "You two should dance. I need to see if I'll be able to move in it. What kind of music are they going to be playing, anyway?"

Grace didn't look away, so neither did he, but she answered her sister. "Some country-western bands. Pretty big names. We have a dance lesson scheduled later today."

"I know how to waltz and two-step." Alex stepped closer and picked up her hand. "Do you?"

"I waltz." They assumed the traditional position of a man and a woman in a ballroom dance, and Alex took the first step.

Grace's voice was as lovely as everything else about her. She counted to three over and over in a little nonsense melody, smiling at him, his beautiful golden girl, silver in his arms, glowing with happiness.

He realized he was smiling back.

So this is happiness. He recognized it, although it had been a very long time since he'd felt it. It was not equilibrium. There was no balance. He was absolutely at the far end of a scale, a feeling of pure pleasure unadulterated by pain—yet.

There was always pain. He knew that, but at this moment, he couldn't imagine ever feeling pain again, not with Grace in his arms.

"One, two, three. One, two, three."

"You look wonderful," the stylist said, clapping. "Sophia, what do you think?"

He and Grace had to stop, or risk looking like fools. She gave his hand a friendly squeeze as she stepped out of his arms. A *friendly* squeeze. Friends. There was pain in being friends with someone he desired so keenly.

"Two things," Sophia announced. "First, you can cancel the dance lesson. He'll do. Second, as pretty as that dress is, I don't think it's for me. Grace should wear it."

For once, Alex thought Sophia was absolutely right.

Grace was less sure. "Me? I couldn't. It's too…gorgeous."

Sophia rolled her eyes impatiently. "Do you have a dress in the suitcase for the ball? No, you do not."

"But I'm not doing the red carpet. I never do."

"That doesn't mean you can wear slacks and a beige sweater. Just take that one. It's pretty, but it's not my style. I'm getting too old for that innocent look. You want me to be more mature, remember?"

The stylist protested. "But the designer provided it for Sophia Jackson. It's a courtesy loan with the understanding it would gain some exposure."

"Tell the designer I'll owe him one next season. Let her wear the dress."

Chapter Seventeen

The dress shone on its hanger, waiting for tomorrow.

Tomorrow.

Time was running out. Tomorrow would be her last day with Alex. He'd traded in this morning's tuxedo for green scrubs and left for the hospital. He was covering someone's half shift in order to have tomorrow off for the Black and White Ball. She could tell he was nonplussed at the concept that it might take an entire day to prepare for five minutes of photographs, but to humor her, he'd traded shifts.

He'd left; Martina had arrived. By the time Martina and the rest of the team had left, Alex's vodka had been poured, declared to be an authentically Russian brand and poured again, and the decision had been made: Sophia and Grace would catch a red-eye back to Los Angeles after the ball. The plan was simple: the press began covering the red carpet at six. Sophia would arrive at seven. The dinner would be served at eight. Sophia would dance with Alex just after nine and then the job was finished. They could strike the set, pack up and go home. *End scene.*

"Wouldn't it be easier to come back to the house and spend one more night?" Grace had asked, feeling that stone in her chest once more.

But the stylists volunteered to pick up their suitcases tomorrow after they stitched her and her sister into their dresses. It was no problem at all for them to take back the gowns and give them their suitcases and send the limo to the airport in plenty of time for a late night flight to the West Coast.

Sophia had pulled her aside and given her the real reason for the rush. "Martina says Deezee is flying in to catch the rest of South by Southwest. I'm not going to be here when he arrives. Haven't you been following his Instagram the last couple of days?"

Grace had not. She'd been out in the sun and fresh air, working shoulder to shoulder with Alex on his days off, trimming peach trees and lemons and figs. She'd worn new garden gloves to handle the cactus, and taken them off to return hugs from great-grandmas at the nursing home. After work, she'd loved watching Alex's hands as he'd whipped up omelets with the same easy dexterity that he must use to tie off a stitch at the hospital.

But they hadn't kissed.

It hadn't been for lack of desire. How many times had their laughter faded away as his gaze fell to her lips? In the silence, she would hold her breath, but he'd turn away. Every time, so far.

If they had more time…but Sophia had decided their time was up.

Grace held her phone and flipped through Deezee's public photos, full of exaggerated pouting expressions and his hands making the shape of a heart over his chest, and she'd understood the red-eye flight. They were running. Whether her sister was running from the possibility of more bad publicity or running away from temptation, Grace wasn't sure.

She only knew one thing for certain: she didn't want to go.

A pane of glass stood between Grace and the man she wanted.

It might as well have been a stone wall.

Alex had returned home from the hospital as darkness fell. Sophia had looked up from her movie and made what was, from her, a friendly overture. "You're going to gag when you hear this medical dialog. Even I can tell it's fake."

Alex had nodded, walked right past her, and headed for the shower.

For half an hour now, he'd been sitting outside in the dark, his hair shower-damp on an evening that was probably a degree too cold for it. Grace thought about bringing him a jacket, but that might make her seem too motherly. She could offer him a cup of hot coffee, but she didn't want to seem like a waitress—or even a personal assistant. She didn't want him to keep seeing her as a friend.

Grace watched him through the sliding glass door, studying the set of his shoulders. He wasn't sitting at the table, but on the edge of the patio, where it dropped off a couple of feet to the garden beyond. His dark hair almost blended into the night.

"You need to fix that."

Grace hadn't realized Sophia was next to her. Now that her sister wasn't wearing the plastic boot, she was as quiet as a cat.

"Fix what?" Grace asked.

"He needs to look like the happiest man in the world when

he stands next to me in less than twenty-four hours, and he's no actor. Go find out what's bugging him. Cheer him up."

"I think we've invaded his personal space enough this week."

In the glass, she watched the reflection of Sophia as she shook her head. "Grace, you're no actress, either. You're dying to go to him. So go."

Grace knew herself. She was going to need a prop to get through this scene. She turned around to pick up her laptop from the couch. "I did make him a little going-away present. Since this is the last time we'll have any peace and quiet, I could show it to him now."

"You're going to go out in the dark to see a man and you're bringing your laptop? What did you make for him? A collage of you in that plunging dress, I hope." Sophia laughed at Grace's scowl. "Take your laptop and do your thing, sis. But trust me—whatever you've got on there isn't what that man really wants. I'm going to bed. See you in the morning."

With her laptop in one hand, Grace slid open the door with her other. Alex turned his head immediately, his profile highlighted by the light that spilled onto the patio from the living room, the handsome angles of his face defined against the black night beyond.

What a pleasure it had been this week to be able to look at him whenever she pleased. Twenty-four hours from now, she might never have that privilege again.

No, no, no...

She set the laptop on the table with a new feeling of determination. She'd give him her gift, and if it worked, she'd have a connection to him, a reason to contact him after she returned to LA.

"Do you mind if I join you?" She rubbed her arms as she strolled over to where he sat on the edge of the patio. Her gray cardigan and blue jeans were warm enough for now, but he'd been outside for a long while. "I could run back inside and grab a jacket for you."

That sounded just as motherly as she'd been afraid it would, the impression made worse by the way she was standing over him. He stopped watching her and turned back to his view of the night.

"Or I could bring you a cup of coffee?" There was the waitress vibe.

Alex gave her some kind of negative-sounding syllable.

She might as well go for broke and add *wife* to the mix. "How was your day at work?"

He stood abruptly and walked a pace into the dark.

She twisted her fingers a bit as she remained on the edge of the patio, watching him. "That bad, huh?"

He turned to look up at her. The soft light illuminated his harsh expression. "I can't talk about specific patients."

"Did somebody die, maybe?"

He shook his head, but it had to have been something almost as bad. The worst thing she'd witnessed in the emergency room had been the violent threats from Mr. Burns to his wife.

That's it. She'd seen Alex with this sharp edge to him once before, in the kitchen in the ER.

"You had to treat another woman like Mrs. Burns," she said quietly.

Alex didn't shake his head

She passionately hated all the misery domestic violence caused. The horror was the worst for the victim, of course, but the effect rippled outward, affecting children and extended family—and the medical personnel who had to deal with the aftermath.

"I'm so sorry. I know you're imagining the best outcome for your patient." Grace felt a hot anger that Alex had to endure that emotional wringer. "At least we'll get that for real with Mr. Burns. I'm telling you, I hope he doesn't take a plea deal. I want to go to his trial. I can't wait to get called to the witness stand."

"No." In one stride, Alex came to stand below her, so intense that he grabbed her hips, his fingers firm through the denim. "I don't want you anywhere near that son of a bitch. If you get called to testify, you tell me. Immediately. Do you understand?"

"Alex." Her heart beat hard at how fiercely protective he was being. He must care for her. He must.

"Burns won't touch you. Not you." His face was inches from her stomach, his hands gripping her hips firmly, and she felt the tension in his every muscle as she set her hands on his shoulders.

She had a second moment of intuition. "It was actually Mrs. Burns again, wasn't it?"

Alex bowed his head. He pressed his forehead to her middle, a moment of intimacy that made her catch her breath. He breathed, too, one strong, swift breath, then another.

Grace clutched his shoulders, then jumped off the ledge to land in the darkness with him. She wanted to be the one to soothe him, but it was he who held her protectively, tucking her head against his shoulder, setting his cheek on her hair—and then, he very gently opened his arms, and stepped away.

She felt a little cold, a little confused. "I'm sorry the happy ending you imagined for her didn't come true."

Alex tucked his hands in the back pockets of his jeans and took another step away from the house. "Everything may still turn out okay for her. It's not that unusual to get pulled back in. Some women get away the second time. Or the third. But they still get away."

"I told you when I first met you that you were an optimist, do you remember?"

He spared her a small smile. He didn't believe her.

Grace tried again. "I'll bet Mrs. Burns was glad you were the doctor on duty. She didn't have to explain anything or try to find a way to speak to someone alone."

"One of us is an optimist, Grace. I think it's you." He kept his hands in his pockets when she wished he would hold her again.

"You don't think she was relieved you were her doctor again?"

There was a beat of silence, barely enough to make her wonder if he was going to answer her.

But he did. "I think she was embarrassed. I know my mother was, when she had to get stitches. Strong women think it shouldn't happen to them, perhaps." He shrugged, as if he hadn't just told her something momentous.

"Your mother? You lived through that as a child?" She'd thought she'd gotten all the important facts during their little interviews. He had no siblings. His parents were divorced. He and his mother had moved from Russia to America when he was fourteen.

None of that was important.

"It only turned physical that last year. There were a few years of tension before that. When the Soviet Union fell apart, so did my parents' marriage. There was an opportunity for the average person to have more say in government, but it was risky. My mother thought it was worth the risk. My father didn't. The arguments escalated every time my mother was jailed. The government was more of a threat to my mother than my father was, but looking back, I think we were escaping both."

When Grace had written down the facts of his youth in her notebook, she'd admired his ability to complete high school in the usual four years despite knowing almost no English the first year.

She'd admired the wrong thing.

"Clark Kent." She sighed the words into the night.

He automatically moved to push up his glasses, but he wasn't wearing them, so he dropped his hand and frowned at her instead.

"It was what I thought when I first saw you. You weren't in awe of my sister. You weren't afraid of Mr. Burns. You even came to the hotel so I wouldn't be intimidated by the police into…into taking an unnecessary risk. Oh, Alex. Thank you."

She took a step toward him. She was dying to touch him. He'd just held her so protectively, but now he seemed so far away.

"Clark Kent isn't far off, is it? You step in to help a lot of people. I am sorry that you're so good at identifying spouse abuse because you witnessed it, though."

"All ER doctors are trained to look for the signs." He put his boot on the ledge and stepped back up to the patio. He turned and offered her his hand to give her a boost up, as well, then smoothly slipped his hand free of hers.

"It must bring up bad memories."

He was silent.

"What do you usually do, when you're home alone after a bad shift?"

"Brood for a little longer, maybe. You snapped me out of it sooner. Thanks."

Something was off here. He was too calm. Too fully recovered when she could still feel where his fingers had dug into the denim waistband of her jeans.

He nodded toward her laptop. "Did you come out here to work?"

She had little choice but to go along with the change of subject. Her crutch had become his. She couldn't drag him back out into the dark.

"It's sort of a thank-you gift for this week." She opened the computer's lid and waited as the screen, too bright in the dark, displayed the first page of her project. "Do you remember that first day when we bought the rocks?"

The day you kissed me like I was the oxygen you needed to breathe?

But there was no sign of that emotion now. No more fierce protectiveness, either. Just…friendliness. Didn't Superman always turn a car right-side up and then fly off alone?

"The manager gave you a couple of extra bags of gravel when he found out what they were for. It started me thinking. If you set up a nonprofit for your landscaping projects, you'd make it easier for a business like that to donate supplies. This is just some brainstorming, but I looked into it, and setting up a nonprofit wouldn't be that complicated."

"Just brainstorming?" He sank into the chair, eyes on the screen as she scrolled down to the table of contents.

"There are grants you'd be eligible for, too. I listed some of them here."

He took over, paging through the mission statement she'd composed, the links to the legal requirements, the proposals she'd written for initial and future workflow. He said nothing until he'd scrolled all the way to the appendix, where she'd created sample spreadsheets he could use for tracking finances and labor.

"This was all inspired by a free bag of rocks?"

"The manager really liked what you were doing. So did I."

Alex nodded, but that harshness had returned to his expression—something about the set of his jaw. "This is what you were doing all those evenings you supposedly weren't working. This is an entire business plan, Grace. We pay people at the hospital to put together grant proposals that aren't as complete as this."

"It's not a big deal," she said, although she wasn't sure why she felt defensive. "I've never had so much free time.

You made sure I didn't work more than nine hours a day, and Sophia stayed in one place for an entire week. This wasn't hard to do."

He shut the lid to the laptop and stood, his physical presence both familiar and intimidating at once. "This takes skill. Don't devalue yourself. Ever."

She fought a shiver. "You keep saying things like that. Like I'm not easily replaced, and I shouldn't let anyone tell me I am. Who said that? Sophia? Martina?"

"You did."

She froze.

Then his calm words started an avalanche of words in her mind. *I'm just doing my job. Why would anyone want to know about me? She could hire a hundred different people to be her assistant.*

Grace felt as light-headed as she did when she skipped a meal. He touched her as he had in the hotel, a firm hand on her upper arm, lending her balance, the touch of a doctor.

His voice was more intimate. "If you could see what I see when I look at you… I want you to believe in yourself. I want to be able to imagine you confident. Please. Be happy."

The unspoken words were loud enough: *when you're gone.* She felt another chill that had nothing to do with the cool night. *I want to imagine you confident when you're gone. Be happy when you're gone.*

He couldn't let her go, never to be seen again. Ten minutes ago, he'd pressed his face into her middle, swearing no harm would come to her. He cared about her.

"I don't want you to imagine me at all. I'm not your patient. We can stay in touch." Grace was no heroine in a movie, but she'd learned this week that she was more courageous than she'd given herself credit for. She dared to touch him, placing one palm on his hard chest, not caring if he could feel the tremor in her hand.

"How long before you go?" The bass in his voice reso-nated through the palm of her hand.

"We leave for the airport right after you dance with Sophia."

He winced. For one second, one precious second, she saw that the loss of her meant so much to him that it caused him pain. The next second, his expression was polite, con-trolled. That poker face was in place, the one he hadn't been using when it was just the two of them.

"The problem is Deezee," she said. "He's coming to Aus-tin, so Sophia is getting out. She's scared to run into him."

His eyes narrowed. "Are you?"

She knew with certainty that if she said *yes*, he would keep her by his side until she felt safe, but she couldn't lie. "Not anymore. There's nothing Deezee can do to hurt me."

"He could come between you and your sister again."

"He can only do that if Sophia lets him. And if she does, I'll be okay without her. I'll still love her, even if she makes a dumb choice."

His scrutiny gave way to a ghost of a smile. "I hope it never comes to that. You and your sister belong together." He let go of her arm and turned toward the house.

He was leaving. She'd just told him this was their last night together, and he was leaving. They were friends, nothing more. Maybe not even that much.

"Wait." Beating down a sense of panic, she scrambled to remember her plan. Her prop. Her crutch—the non-profit information—she opened the laptop again. "I need your email address. I'll send the business plan to you. And then…and then you could appoint me to the board. There only needs to be three of us. I'll be your secretary. Be-tween the phone and email, it would be no problem at all for me to do the bookkeeping and get grant applications ready, even when I'm out of state."

And I'll have an excuse to call you when I want to hear your voice.

"No."

She felt all the air go out of her chest. Out of her world.

"I'm sorry, Grace, but no. I don't want to continue on that way. Not being together, but not falling completely out of touch, just in case our paths cross again."

Tears stung her eyes and clogged her throat. He didn't want to stay in touch with her, not at all. They weren't really friends.

"It's what you were thinking, wasn't it? Maybe you'll be back next year for South-by. Maybe your sister will come back to film a sequel to whatever she filmed here last September. Maybe…" He set his hands on his hips and looked out at the dark garden, shaking that perfectly cut hair back from his perfectly blue eyes. "Maybe Burns will go to trial, and we'll catch dinner while you're in town. I don't do that, Grace. I can't be on call for you. I'm not that man."

"Then what man are you?"

"Not the kind that dates the personal assistant of a movie star."

That sounded so final. She *was* the sister of a movie star. She couldn't change that. "I thought you and Sophia were teasing each other, mostly. Do you really not like her?"

Do you hate my sister the way Deezee hates me?

She had his attention, at least. He looked from the dark back to her, mildly surprised. "I've got a newfound respect for her this week, actually. She's chosen a difficult career, but she's loyal to you. That's the most important thing."

Wrong. Having more time with you is the most important thing. But she wasn't quite enough of a superhero to say such a thing.

"So if it's not the movie star, then it's me. The girl with no friends. The girl who's afraid to say her sister's name in public. I know that's not normal."

But he was shaking his head. "I'm no judge of normal. You and your sister were together during the toughest time of your life, and now you're never apart. My mother and I were together during the toughest time of our lives, and we hardly see each other. Which of us is normal, Grace? You get your stability from another human being, at least. I spend my time with rocks."

"You spend your time making beautiful gardens for people."

"Ah, Grace. *Milost'.*"

He touched her, smoothing his hand over her hair. She couldn't mock herself for being so hyperaware as he touched her hair, for she felt it as acutely as if he'd slid his hand over her breast.

He's going to kiss me.

His gaze moved from her hair to her mouth, but he didn't lean in, didn't give in, to what she knew he wanted. She waited, anticipating, but his look of want was replaced by that poker face once more.

"We should get some sleep," he said, dropping his hand to his side, all business now. "What time in the morning are the first people—"

She silenced him with her kiss, her mouth, desperate to erase that neutral expression and snap that calm control. His lips were warm and surprisingly soft and seriously strong. It was so wonderful, such a relief to be kissing the man she'd been so attuned to all week, that it took her long, blissful moments before she realized that while he was kissing her back, he wasn't taking over. He wasn't letting the kiss take over, either. He allowed nothing to burn out of control—it was nothing like that kiss by the truck.

She became aware of this as she became aware that she was nearly on her toes, pressed against him, her soft chest against his harder one, her hands once more clutching his shoulders.

His hands weren't on her.

She ended the kiss and stood solidly on her feet once more.

"I thought... I thought I meant more to you." Grace knew, somewhere in her objective mind, that she ought to feel embarrassed. But Alex was so calm, so unaffected, that she felt a little bitter. "You said everything you did this week was to help me. You said you had my back."

"I'm still backing you up. I'll be spending all day tomorrow backing you up."

"Until I get on that plane. Then that's it, isn't it?"

Her heart broke as he nodded.

The bitterness became huge. "I didn't realize your friendship had an expiration date."

"I always knew you were leaving in a week. You knew it, too, Grace. That's why we never let anything go too far."

"We didn't? *We?* Did you really think I didn't want to kiss you every single day?" Tears stung her eyes, born of embarrassment that he hadn't been swept away by her kiss—or perhaps the tears were simply because it hurt to hear him say he'd never planned to see her after this week. Or perhaps it was worse than that.

Perhaps she was in love.

Tears fell. The man she loved was going to walk out of her life.

How puny all her wishes this week had been, wasted on wanting to stay away from LA, wasted on wanting a dumb DJ to leave her alone, as if geography and her sister's affairs mattered as much as Alex. She loved him, but he was leaving her.

I wish you loved me, too.

Alex pushed her hair away from her face, his warm hand lingering on her cheek. "You started this week by saying it was a mistake when we kissed. I thought you were being smart. We won't miss what we've never had."

"But we don't have to miss each other. I can visit you here. You can fly out to California."

"For what? To spend a day or two together?" His hand stayed gentle but the look in his eyes turned almost angry. "Some sex, a few dinners. A long weekend here, a holiday there. It's not enough, Grace. It's going to be hell watching you disappear tomorrow. Don't ask me to live through a dozen more disappearances in the future. I meant it when I said I'm not that man."

"Then I don't know what to do," she said, closing her eyes against the intensity in his, "because you're the only man for me."

The silence was electric, then his hand on her cheek was cupping the back of her head instead, pulling her close as he kissed her, hungry this time. Starving. His arm came around her as he opened her mouth with his own, and the slide of his tongue made her whimper with pleasure. He was delicious. He kissed her as if *she* were delicious, and she felt herself melting with each slow, strong taste. She held on to his arms, felt his muscles bunching as he slid his hand over her backside, lifting her higher against his hard body. The intimacy of their kiss, the sure touch of his hands—everything between them was so gloriously hot in the cold night.

Then he tore his mouth away, and she was left dizzy and disoriented once more, clinging to his arms. He was breathing as hard as she was, uneven, uncontrolled. Still hungry.

"That was not a mistake," she panted.

"It was for me."

Alex let her go, and disappeared into his own house.

Chapter Eighteen

Alex lay on his couch, staring into the dark, obsessed with the woman in his bed.

He should never have kissed Grace. She felt like forever in his arms; she was leaving. In hours.

Some last scrap of self-preservation had kicked in, and he'd broken off that kiss before it had turned into more. He'd headed straight for his bedroom—alone—to pitch his jeans and shirt into the laundry basket and pull on a pair of loose track pants, and to hell with a shirt. Then he'd settled in for one last night on this couch as if he weren't aware that Grace Jackson was still on his back porch, staring at her laptop with a look of misery on her beautiful face.

It was cold out there. He'd been just about to throw off his blanket and bring it out to her when she'd come in and headed straight for the bedroom herself.

The house was silent now. Dark. It was impossible not to relive the kiss that had guaranteed that this last night would be just like the first: sleepless and full of sexual frustration.

He threw off the blanket and headed for the kitchen. The refrigerator light blinded him. The cold milk chilled him to the bone, but he drank it anyway, all of it, straight from the carton, wishing it would numb his brain.

Grace Jackson. One week with her and his life would never be the same. And what did she want from him? To be her pen pal. They'd play at setting up a nonprofit and send each other e-mails.

He tossed the carton onto the counter in disgust.

"I can't sleep, either."

Grace's voice was gentle behind him. He knew how she'd look if he turned around. Barefooted. White pajamas. Irresistible.

He turned around, anyway.

You look very, very beautiful.

The thick satin wasn't as modest as she probably thought it was. It was not sheer, but it molded every curve, from the roundness of her shoulder to the peak of her breast. The impact she had on him was so much more than body parts. She was a complete person, not merely luscious but full of life. She was anxious only in her desire to help others, generous with her time and determined to be optimistic, with hope in her brown eyes and a halo when light touched her hair. She was Grace—and he knew, in the low glow of the kitchen clock, he was in love with her.

She opened her palm and offered him a USB flash drive. "It's got the business plan on it. Even if I'm not part of the project, you still might want to use it."

He didn't move. He couldn't, because the only move possible was to crush her in his arms, to claim her as his own, as if tomorrow wouldn't come and she wouldn't fly a thousand miles away.

His eyes were too well adjusted. He could see the hurt on her face when he didn't reach for the small stick.

She closed her fist around it—and stepped closer to him.

"That first kiss, at the barbecue place, that was the best kiss of my life. When you never kissed me again, I thought it must not have been that amazing to you. Maybe you just weren't that into me. But then tonight…" She let her fingers trail along his waistband as she had that first night, her touch less tentative now. "Out there on the patio, you didn't kiss me like a man who's not that into me."

His stomach contracted, his arousal hardened, and he fought to remember that the woman he loved was only passing through. She'd be gone tomorrow.

I can't. She'd said that the first night. *I can't, I can't.* Then she'd run away. Tonight, she smoothed her empty hand up his chest.

He had nowhere to run.

"While I was packing, I told myself maybe tonight was only physical. Maybe you and I just happen to be physically compatible. You kissed me tonight like you wanted to take me to bed. A lot of guys would take what a willing woman offered."

While she was packing. She'd thought through these possibilities while she was packing. To leave him.

Grace slid her hand over his shoulder, then erased the last of the distance between them by putting both arms around his neck. The move was as confident as a siren's, but the look in her eyes was too vulnerable, as if she thought he might possibly be able to resist the dark and the satin and the sincerity.

He could not. His hands circled her waist, sliding the satin up so his palms warmed her skin. No more, just that.

She shook back her dark gold hair. "If you only wanted

sex, you could have taken me to bed every night this week. You know I would have gone willingly."

Never had he been so tempted in his life. He pushed himself away and turned his back on her, then drove a hand through his own hair.

"But you didn't." She sounded sad, like a woman who'd been rejected. Damn it, he felt guilty for not scooping her up and throwing her on his bed.

It's not you, it's me.

"So I think you aren't that kind of guy. I think you want an emotional connection before you take a woman to bed. But you know what? We do have an emotional connection. So there I was, folding my clothes and putting them in my suitcase, and I thought about Mrs. Burns."

Surprised, he turned around.

"You told me you rarely see the same patient twice. Until tonight, I hadn't realized that was a good thing for you. No one goes to the ER because they are well and happy. If you see them again, it's bad. Like Mrs. Burns. Of course you never want to see people again. It's so much better to assume they are doing fine without you. It gives you peace of mind when they don't return."

She paused to take a breath. He was already holding his.

"That's your life, isn't it? People come in. You help them. They leave."

He exhaled, a sharp hiss of a sound because she'd cut right down to the problem with surgical precision.

"And now I'm leaving tomorrow, too." She took his hand and pressed the plastic stick into his palm. "My phone number is on that flash drive. Call me."

Not pen pals, then, but phone-a-friends. He would still be burning for her, while she would still be living her sister's life in LA or New York or Tunisia or any of the places she'd told him about this week.

When he didn't close his fist around the stick, she closed his fingers over it herself. She had tears in her eyes.

Alex hated being the one who'd put those tears in her eyes. The sooner he could make her understand, the sooner she would resume her life without him. "You'll be fine without me. I thought you needed me to slay a few dragons for you this week. You didn't. You've got everything it takes to slay those dragons yourself. You always did."

"What dragons?"

He had to shake his head at his own mistaken assumptions. "Your sister seemed manipulative. You were so anxious to avoid going back to California. I jumped to conclusions, but now I've seen how you can hold your own. More than that. You are very good at your job. You never needed me."

"I did need you. I needed a friend desperately. I still do."

"You need a man who doesn't give a damn about some idiot DJ in Los Angeles to wear a tux tomorrow. When you leave, you're going to be fine. You're a very strong person."

"You're determined to imagine me living a good life without you, aren't you?" She gripped his fist in both of her hands. "Don't you dare imagine that."

There was nothing fragile or delicate in her touch. It was as if his compliments had made her furious.

"It won't be true. I'm going to be missing you, Alex, every day. That's not a pleasant way to live. I'm going to be imagining you building gardens all alone, and I'm going to wonder if you wished you had my help. But the worst thing of all, the thing that's really going to leave me gutted, is that I'm going to wonder if each day was the day that you saw Mrs. Burns a third time. I'm going to wonder if you are sitting alone on your patio with no one to talk to."

Her anger didn't stop her tears from falling. Each one hurt as if it were his own. He'd messed everything up so badly, falling hard for a woman who hadn't had the good sense to see that he wasn't the right man for her.

"I'm sorry," she said, subdued. "It's not normal to never see people again, and it breaks my heart to know you've trained yourself to live as though it is. If a long-distance lover is too unstable for you, I could still be your friend. I want you to see what it's like to have someone you can call. So call me."

She squeezed his fist once more, pressing the hard stick more deeply into his palm, and then she let go and began backing away. "Just call me, if you can. If you want to. I want you to. Good night."

She disappeared down the hall, an angel gone in a flash of white.

No.

He couldn't let it end this way. She was leaving—didn't the pain always come?—but she wasn't going to disappear entirely. She understood him and the reasons he craved stability, and she was offering him as much as she thought he could handle. Having a friend to call after a hard, painful day would be a new experience for him. Yes, she was leaving, but she was throwing him this one thread, this one connection. It would be a giant step outside his comfort zone, but she thought he could do it.

No, she *needed* him to do it. If he didn't call her, she'd be unhappy. He was that important to her. He mattered to her, and the sweetness of it pierced his heart. It would hurt him to hear her voice and have nothing else, but if it would hurt her more not to have any connection, then he'd do it. For her, he could do anything, because he loved her.

He strode into his own bedroom. She was standing by the bed, her open suitcase an ominous sight on the comforter.

"Grace." He captured her face in his hands. "Yes, I will call you. Every damned day that you're gone, I'll call you."

"Every day?" He'd startled her, but the hope was clear in her eyes.

"I don't know how to do this, but I'll find a way."

"How to talk every day? I'll do all the talking, if you don't know what to say. I would love to talk to you every day."

"If we can only be friends on the phone, then I'll take it, but Grace, I am in love with you. I have been since you shoved your arm in that kitchen door, I think, so determined to make me listen. I don't know how to live with part of you, when what I want is all of you, but I'll figure it out."

Because he was in love with her, he had to kiss her, a hard kiss—a swift kiss, because more words needed to be said as he kept her precious face in his hands. "You were right then, and you were right tonight. I let go of too many people, my patients, my friends, even my mother, when they didn't need me. You may not need me, Grace, but I need you. It's going to hurt like hell when we're apart, but for once in my life, I'm keeping someone I love."

"I don't want to settle for friends on the phone, either. I love you, too, Alex."

There were tears in her eyes again, but this time, his heart didn't hurt when they fell. He wiped them away with his thumbs.

"I have to leave tomorrow, but I'll come back. As soon as I possibly can, I'll be back, Alex. I promise."

God, she loved him. He wanted to hear her say it again, but she was kissing him, and it felt too perfect to stop. Her touch at his waist was bold. She slid her hand into his waistband and used it to pull him with her as she lowered herself onto the bed, stretching out sideways beside the hated suitcase. He followed, sheer desire threatening to obliterate every other thought. Her hair, her skin, her hands on his body—the effort it took to get back up from the bed was monstrous.

Grace sat up, confused. "You don't want…"

Alex almost laughed. "I've never wanted anything more." He picked up her suitcase and set it on the floor, went to the bedroom door and shut it firmly. Then he stood over Grace a moment, taking in her beauty.

He scooped his arms around her and moved her with him to the center of the bed. "Come here, beautiful."

"Oh," Grace said, a little sound of relief as she slid one satin-clad leg over his. "You said it was hard to miss what you'd never had, so I thought for a moment that maybe you didn't want to have this, so you wouldn't miss it tomorrow."

It was their first time to be horizontal together, the first time she could nuzzle her face into the side of his neck.

"I'm going to miss you, anyway," he said, his voice rough with the truth of it. Their clothes allowed him to keep some shred of control as he rolled onto his back and lifted her to lie atop him. Her knees slid to either side of his hips, the first time of countless times to come. He gritted his teeth against the sharp spike of desire, and ignored the looming pain of tomorrow.

The first time of countless times. He'd find a way to make that true.

Grace sat up, straddling him, unbuttoning the first white button. "Then I guess we should find out exactly what we'll be missing."

The chauffeur opened the limousine door.

Grace stayed on the bench seat, out of the way of the open door and the paparazzi's cameras. Alex stepped out, looking less like Clark Kent and more like James Bond as he popped his cuffs and buttoned his jacket. Then he reached a hand into the limousine to assist Sophia Jackson onto the red carpet.

Her sister had decided to wear white at the last minute. Grace leaned forward to give the train of the gown a flip as Sophia exited the limo, so she and Alex looked perfect as they walked up the first shallow steps to the photographer's area.

The chauffeur handed Grace out. She carried her purse and Sophia's, and walked quietly along the edge of the carpet, the silent signal to the organizers that she was an assistant, not to be photographed or fussed over despite her silver designer dress and her obviously professional hair and makeup.

Sophia said something to Alex, then started walking toward Grace. Grace actually turned to see who might be behind her. "What are you doing, Sophie?"

"We've never done pictures as sisters. Don't protest. That silver dress is the bomb."

For the first time, Grace found herself arm in arm with her sister, strolling to the center of the red carpet, smiling at the barrage of camera flashes. The rhythm of it came naturally after watching Sophia do it for years—look left, center, right, pausing for just enough seconds that it felt awkward—then they turned toward the stairs, and Alex escorted them with one sister on each arm.

That hadn't been the plan. Grace hoped Sophia knew what she was doing. This little threesome would only raise speculation. Which sister was Alex escorting?

Their happy family group turned back into a twosome as Alex and Sophia took their places at a reserved table at the front of the ballroom. Grace, like the good personal assistant she was, slipped a white purse to her sister. "Your cellphone and lipstick are in there, safety pins and bobby pins."

As she turned to leave, Sophia caught her hand. "Thanks, Grace. You really are the best."

Well, okay. That seemed a little intense for a few pins, but Grace smiled and then concentrated on winding her way to the very back of the ballroom. Her dress was too valuable to let it get caught or stepped on, so she was absorbed in avoiding chairs, sidestepping waiters with their heavy trays, turning sideways to pass other women in gowns, and dodging Deezee Kalm as he came barreling past her, running toward the front of the room.

Deezee Kalm!

Grace whirled around and started fighting her way back to her sister's table. The going was harder, because everyone was pushing back their chairs and standing to see what was happening. Deezee made it easier for them by leaping onto the center of her sister's dinner table, planting his high-top sneakers right where the salads and rolls sat, a filthy, asinine, attention-getting move.

"Excuse me," Grace said over and over, pushing her way to her sister. Her dress would have to survive the crush. "Excuse me."

Grace broke through the crowd as Deezee dropped dramatically to one knee. Since he was on the table, he was still above Sophia, not exactly the humble pose of a man about to propose. Alex had Sophia tucked behind his back protectively, but Sophia looked ecstatic, positively glowing with excitement.

"Run away with me." Deezee held out his hand, more of a demand than a plea. "Right now, baby. Let's go. I've got a private jet waiting. Just you and me on a tropical island, away from all this crap."

Sophia sidestepped Alex and placed her hand in Deezee's. "You want to marry me right now?"

"Sure, girl. Let's go crazy."

"That was crazy." Grace looked out the limousine window at the Austin city lights.

Alex held her hand. "Are you okay?"

"I suppose so. I'm not really hurt. Sophie just wants to be happy. I'm just afraid that Deezee isn't the man who is really going to make her happy."

"We could be wrong."

Grace put her head on Alex's shoulder. "Martina set it up yesterday. I should have known there was a reason Sophie switched to that white gown. I know this isn't important, but I always assumed I'd be her maid of honor. I guess that's not going to happen."

Alex dropped a kiss on her very fancy hair. "Maybe that's why she wanted those photos with you tonight. She knew she was in her wedding gown."

"And this is my bridesmaid's dress?" Grace sat up and turned to face Alex. "If you're trying to make me feel better, you're succeeding."

She wanted to talk to him about everything, but the limousine was moving toward the airport, and her time was short. She took her cellphone out of her silver purse, her prop for this talk. "I have something to show you. It's Sophia's boarding pass to get on the plane tonight."

Alex watched her as she swiped her finger over the screen.

"But here's mine. It's cancelled. I'm not going to back to LA tonight."

Alex looked truly stunned.

"Some woman named Jackson was supposed to spend a week making love to her new man in Texas, so I thought it might as well be me. I told Sophia today I was taking some long overdue vacation days."

Alex started to laugh as he reached into his inner jacket pocket and pulled out his cell phone. "Let me show you something. This is my boarding pass. I decided if I couldn't stand to be apart from you, then I ought to stay with you. I was going to be on your flight to LA tonight. I arranged with the other doctors to take my long overdue vacation."

"Oh, my gosh. What should we do?"

Alex raised one eyebrow at her. "We should take a vacation."

Grace wanted to cuddle that digital boarding pass on his cellphone to her chest like the treasure it was. It gave her courage. "I've been thinking more long-term. When Sophia gets back from her trip, I told her I'd help her interview new assistants. I'm ready to live my own life."

Alex said nothing.

Grace held on to her courage. "Conventional wisdom says I should take some time to adjust. I should get a job and think only about myself for a while."

"You're probably right about that."

It was a terribly neutral answer, but Alex was watching her closely, intently listening to every word she had to say. He wasn't neutral at all when it came to her.

There was no time like the present—no time like a private limo ride in a silver gown to proposition a man in a tuxedo.

"But here's what I really want to do, in my heart. I'm good at being a couple. I like living with someone else. It's too much, too soon, everyone will say, but I'm afraid I'm going to miss seeing your face. I love being around you. I love having you for a friend. I don't want to be clingy or dependent, but I want to live with you." She came to a stop, choked up by emotion and afraid she was babbling.

Alex looked so terribly serious as he picked up her hand. "When it comes to living together, I'm afraid that all I can do is offer you all or nothing."

"Oh." Grace could feel her heart pounding hard. She didn't know quite what he meant.

"I can love you like that, but it would have to be for keeps. I couldn't handle living together for a few weeks or a few months or a few years, only to have you disappear. It would have to be forever, Grace."

"I can do forever." But she looked at him cautiously, unsure of his mood. He was so very grave.

"Good, because that's the kind of man I am." Then he reached in the pocket of his jacket once more, and her heart tripped in a seriously happy dance of anticipation. "I bought something today. I was prepared to carry it with me until you were sure of what you wanted, no matter how long that took. I should have known you already had a plan. The best plan. The only plan for us."

"Oh, Alex. Are we really going to do this?"

He pulled out a diamond ring and smiled at her, the most intimate, perfect smile a man has ever given a woman.

"Yes, Grace. We're really going to do this. Together. Forever."

* * * * *

Will Sophie Jackson ever find love?
Don't miss her story, next in
Caro Carson's
TEXAS RESCUE miniseries,
coming in December 2016 from
Harlequin Special Edition!

Drake Carson is willing to put up with Luce Hale, the supposed "expert" his mother brought to the ranch, as long as she can get the herd of wild horses off his land, but the pretty academic wants to study them instead! Sparks are sure to fly when opposites collide in Mustang Creek...

Read on for a sneak peek from New York Times *bestselling author Linda Lael Miller's second book in* THE CARSONS OF MUSTANG CREEK *trilogy,* ALWAYS A COWBOY, *coming September 2016 from HQN Books.*

CHAPTER ONE

THE WEATHER JUST plain sucked, but that was okay with Drake Carson. In his opinion, rain was better than snow any day of the week, and as for sleet... Well, that was wicked, especially in the wide-open spaces, coming at a person in stinging blasts like a barrage of buckshot. Yep, give him a slow, gentle rainfall every time, the kind that generally meant spring was in the works. Anyhow, he could stand to get a little wet. Here in Wyoming, this close to the mountains, the month of May might bring sunshine and pastures blanketed with wildflowers, but it could also mean a rogue snowstorm fit to bury folks and critters alike.

Raising his coat collar around his ears, he nudged his horse into motion with his heels. Starburst obeyed, although he seemed hesitant about it, even edgy, and Drake wondered why. For almost a year now, livestock had gone missing—mostly calves, but the occasional steer or heifer, too. While it didn't happen often, for a rancher, a single lost animal was one too many. The spread was big, and he couldn't keep an eye on the whole place at once, of course.

He sure as hell tried, though.

"Stay with me," he told his dogs, Harold and Violet, a pair of German shepherds from the same litter and some of the best friends he'd ever had.

Then, tightening the reins slightly, in case Starburst took a notion to bolt out of his easy trot, he looked around, narrowing his eyes to see through the downpour. Whatever he'd expected to spot—a grizzly or a wildcat or a band of modern-day rustlers, maybe—he *hadn't* expected a lone female just up ahead, crouched behind a small tree and clearly drenched, despite the dark rain slicker covering her slender form.

She was peering through a pair of binoculars, having taken no apparent notice of Drake, his dogs or his horse. Even with the rain pounding down, they should have been hard to miss, being only fifty yards away.

Whoever this woman might be, she wasn't a neighbor or a local, either. Drake would have recognized her if she'd lived in or around Mustang Creek, and the whole ranch was posted against trespassers, mainly to keep tourists out. A lot of visiting sightseers had seen a few too many G-rated animal movies, and thought they could cozy up to a bear, a bison or a wolf for a selfie to post on social media.

Most times, if the damn fools managed to get away alive, they were missing a few body parts or the family pet.

Drake shook off the images and concentrated on the subject at hand—the woman in the rain slicker.

Who was she, and what was she doing on Carson property?

A stranger, yes.

But it dawned on Drake that, whatever else she might be, she *wasn't* the reason his big Appaloosa was suddenly so skittish.

The woman was fixated on the wide meadow, actually a shallow valley, just beyond the copse of cottonwood, and so, Drake realized now, was Starburst.

He stood in his stirrups and squinted, and his heart picked up speed as he caught sight—finally—of the band of wild mustangs grazing there. Once numbering only half a dozen or so, the herd had grown to more than twenty.

Now, alerted by the stallion, their leader and the un-
qualified bane of Drake's existence, they scattered.

He was vigilant, that devil on four feet, and cocky, too.

He lingered for a few moments, while the mares fled
in the opposite direction, tossed his magnificent head and
snorted.

Too late, sucker.

Drake cursed under his breath and promptly forgot all
about the woman who shouldn't have been there in the
first damn place, his mind on the expensive mare—make
that *mares*—the stallion had stolen from him. He whistled
through his teeth, the piercing whistle that brought tame
horses running, ready for hay, a little sweet feed and a
warm stall.

He hadn't managed to get this close to the stallion and
his growing harem in a long while, and he hated to let the
opportunity pass, but he knew that if he gave chase, the
dogs would be right there with him, and probably wind up
getting their heads kicked in.

The stallion whinnied, taunting him, and sped away,
topping the rise on the other side of the meadow and van-
ishing with the rest.

The dogs whimpered, itching to run after them, but
Drake ordered them to stay; then he whipped off his hat,
rain be damned, and smacked it hard against his thigh in
pure exasperation. This time, he cussed in earnest.

Harold and Violet were fast and they were agile, but
he'd raised them from pups and he couldn't risk letting
them get hurt.

Hope stirred briefly when Drake's prize chestnut quar-
ter horse, a two-year-old mare destined for greatness, re-
appeared at the crest of the hill opposite, ears pricked at
the familiar whistle, but the stallion came back for her,

crowding her, nipping at her neck and flanks, and then she was gone again.

Damn it all to hell.

"Thanks for nothing, mister."

It was the intruder, the trespasser. The woman stormed toward Drake through the rain-bent grass, waving the binoculars like a maestro raising a baton at the symphony. If he hadn't been so annoyed by her mere presence, let alone her nerve—yelling at him like that when *she* was the one in the wrong—he might have been amused.

She was a sight for sure, plowing through the grass, all fuss and fury and wet to the skin.

Mildly curious now that the rush of adrenaline roused by losing another round to that son-of-a-bitching stallion was beginning to subside, Drake waited with what was, for him, uncommon patience. He hoped the approaching tornado, pint-size but definitely category five, wouldn't step on a snake before she completed the charge.

Born and raised on this land, he wouldn't have stomped around like that, not without keeping a close eye out for rattlers.

As she got closer, he made out an oval face, framed by the hood of her coat, and a pair of amber eyes that flashed as she demanded, "Do you have any idea how long it took me to get that close to those horses? Days! And what happens? *You* have to come along and ruin everything!"

Drake resettled his hat, tugging hard at the brim, and waited.

The woman all but stamped her feet. "Days!" she repeated wildly.

Drake felt his mouth twitch. "Excuse me, ma'am, I'm a bit confused. You're here because…?"

"Because of the horses!" The tone and pitch of her voice

said he was an idiot for even asking. Apparently he ought to be able to read her mind instead.

He gave himself points for politeness—and for managing a reasonable tone. "I see," he said, although of course he didn't.

"The least you could do is apologize," she informed him, glaring.

Still mounted, Drake adjusted his hat again. The dogs sat on either side of him and Starburst, staring at the woman as if she'd sprung up out of the ground.

When he replied, he sounded downright amiable. In his own opinion, anyway. "Apologize? Now, why would I do that? Given that I *live* here, I mean. This is private property, Ms.—"

She wasn't at all fazed to find out that she was on somebody else's land, uninvited. Nor did she offer her name.

"It took me hours to track those horses down," she ranted on, still acting like the offended party, "in this weather, no less! I finally get close enough, and you—you..." She paused, but only to suck in a breath so she could go right on strafing him with words. "*You* try hiding behind a tree without moving a muscle, waiting practically forever, and with water dripping down your neck."

He might have pointed out that he was no stranger to inclement weather, since he rode fence lines in blizzards and rounded up strays under a hot sun—and those were the *easy* days—but he refrained. "What were you doing there, behind my tree?"

"*Your* tree? No one owns a tree."

"Maybe not, but people can own the ground it grows on. And that's the case here, I'm afraid."

She rolled her eyes.

Great, a tree hugger. She probably drove one of those

little hybrid cars, plastered with bumper stickers, and cruised along at thirty miles an hour in the left lane.

Nobody loved nature more than he did, but hell, the Carsons had held the deed to this ranch for more than a century, and it wasn't a public campground with hiking trails, nor was it a state park.

Drake leaned forward in the saddle. "Do the words *no trespassing* mean anything to you?" he asked sternly.

On some level, though, he was enjoying this encounter way more than he should have.

She merely glowered up at him, arms folded, chin raised.

He sighed. "All right. Let's see if we can clarify matters. That tree—" he gestured to the one she'd taken refuge behind earlier, and spoke very slowly so she'd catch his drift "—is on land my family owns. I'm Drake Carson. And you are?"

The look of surprise on her face was gratifying. "*You're* Drake Carson?"

"I was when I woke up this morning," he said in a deliberate drawl. "I don't imagine that's changed since then." A measured pause. "Now, how about answering my original question? What are you doing here?"

She seemed to wilt, and Drake supposed that was a victory, however small, but he wasn't inclined to celebrate. "I'm studying the horses."

The brim of his hat spilled water down his front as he nodded. "Well, yeah, I kind of figured that. It's really not the point, now, is it? Like I said, this is private property. And if you'd asked permission to be here, I'd know it."

She blushed, but no explanation was forthcoming. "So you're *him*."

"Yes, ma'am. You—"

The next moment, she was blustering again. "Tall man on a tall horse," she remarked, her tone scathing.

A few seconds earlier, he'd been in charge here. Now he felt defensive, which was ridiculous.

He drew a deep breath, released it slowly and spoke with quiet authority. He hoped. "My height and my horse have nothing to do with anything, as far as I can see. My point, once again, is you don't have the right to be here, much less yell at me."

"Yes, I do."

Of all the freaking gall. Drake glowered at the young woman standing next to his horse by then, unafraid, giving as good as she got. "What?"

"I *do* have the right to be here," she insisted. "I asked your mother's permission to come out and study the wild horses, and she said yes. In fact, she was very supportive."

Well, shit.

Would've been nice if his mother had bothered to mention it to him.

For some reason, he couldn't back off, or not completely, anyway. Call it male pride. "Okay," he said evenly. "*Why* do you want to study wild horses? Considering that they're...*wild* and everything."

She seemed thoroughly undaunted. "I'm doing my graduate thesis on how wild horses exist and interact with domesticated animals on working ranches." She added with emphasis, "And how ranchers deal with them. Like you."

So he was part of the equation. Yippee.

"Just so you understand," he said, "you aren't going to study *me*."

"What if I got your mother's permission?" she asked sweetly.

"Very funny." By then, Drake's mood was headed straight downhill. What was he doing out here in the damn rain, bantering with some self-proclaimed intellectual, when all he'd had before leaving the house this morning was a skimpy breakfast and one cup of coffee? The saddle leather creaked as he bent toward her. "Listen, Ms. Whoever-you-are, I don't give a rat's ass about your thesis, or your theories about ranchers and wild horses, either. Do what you have to do, try not to get yourself killed and then move on to whatever's next on your agenda—preferably elsewhere."

Not surprisingly, the woman wasn't intimidated. "Hale," she announced brightly. "My name is Lucinda Hale, but everybody calls me Luce."

He inhaled, a long, deep breath. If he'd ever had that much trouble learning a woman's name before, he didn't recall the occasion. "Ms. Hale, then," he began, tugging at the brim of his hat in a gesture that was more automatic than cordial. "I'll leave you to it. While I'm sure your work is absolutely fascinating, I have plenty of my own to do. In short, while I've enjoyed shadowboxing with you, I'm fresh out of leisure time."

He might've been talking to a wall. "Oh, don't worry," she said cheerfully. "I wouldn't *dream* of interfering. I'll be an observer, that's all. Watching, figuring out how things work, making a few notes. You won't even know I'm around."

Drake sighed inwardly and reined his horse away, although he didn't use his heels. The dogs, still fascinated by the whole scenario, sat tight. "You're right, Ms. Hale. I won't know you're around, because you won't be. Around *me*, that is."

"You really are a very difficult man," she observed almost sadly. "Surely you can see the value of my project. Interactions between wild animals, domesticated ones and human beings?"

LUCE WAS COLD, wet, a little amused and *very* intrigued.

Drake Carson was gawking at her as though she'd just popped in from a neighboring dimension, wearing a tutu and waving a wand. His two beautiful dogs, waiting obediently for some signal from their master, seemed equally curious.

The consternation on his face was absolutely priceless.

And a very handsome face it was, at least what she could see of it in the shadow of his hat brim. If he had the same features as his younger brother Mace, whom she'd met earlier that day, he was one very good-looking man.

She decided to push him a bit further. "You run this ranch, don't you?"

"I do my best."

She liked his voice, which was calm and carried a low drawl. "Then you're the one I want."

Oh, no, she thought, that came out all wrong.

"For my project, I mean."

His strong jawline tightened visibly. "I don't have time to babysit you," he said. "This is a working ranch, not a resort."

"As I've said repeatedly, Mr. Carson, you won't have to do anything of the sort. I can take care of myself, and I'll stay out of your way as much as possible."

He seemed unconvinced. Even irritated.

But he didn't ride away.

Luce had already been warned that he wouldn't take to her project.

Talk about an understatement.

Mentally, she cataloged the things she'd learned about Drake Carson.

He was in charge of the ranch, which spanned thousands of acres and was home to lots of cattle and horses, as well as wildlife. The Carsons had very deep ties to

Bliss County, Wyoming, going back several generations. He loved the outdoors, was good with animals, especially horses.

He was, in fact, a true cowboy.

He was also on the quiet side, solitary by nature, slow to anger—but watch out if he did. At thirty-two, Drake had never been married; he was college-educated, and once he'd gotten his degree, he'd come straight back to the ranch, having no desire to live anywhere else. He worked from sunrise to sunset and often longer.

Harry, the housekeeper whose real name was Harriet Armstrong, had dished up some sort of heavenly pie when Luce had arrived at the main ranch house, fairly early in the day. As soon as she understood who Luce was and why she was there, she'd proceeded to spill information about Drake at a steady clip.

Luce had encountered Mace Carson, Drake's younger brother, very briefly, when he'd come in from the family vineyard expressly for a piece of pie. Harry had introduced them and explained Luce's mission—i.e., to gather material for her thesis and interview Drake in depth, and get the rancher's perspective.

Mace had smiled slightly and shaken his head in response. "I'm glad you're here, Ms. Hale, but I'm afraid my brother isn't going to be a whole lot of use as a research subject. He's into his work and not much else, and he doesn't like to be distracted from it. Makes him testy."

A quick glance in Harry's direction had confirmed the sinking sensation created by Mace's words. The other woman had given a small, reluctant nod of agreement.

Well, Luce thought now, standing face-to-horse with Drake, they'd certainly known what they were talking about.

Drake was *definitely* testy.

He stared grimly into the rainy distance for a long

moment, then muttered, "As if that damn stallion wasn't enough to get under my skin—"

"Cheer up," Luce said. She loved a challenge. "I'm here to help."

Drake gave her a long, level look. "Why didn't you say so in the first place?" he drawled, without a hint of humor. He flung out his free hand for emphasis, the reins resting easily in the other one. "My problems are over."

"Didn't you tell me you were leaving?" Luce asked.

He opened his mouth, closed it again, evidently reconsidering whatever he'd been about to say. Finally, with a mildly defensive note in his voice, he went on. "I planned to," he said, "but if I did, you'd be out here alone." He looked around. "Where's your horse? You won't be getting close to those critters again today. The stallion will see to that."

Luce's interest was genuine. "You sound as if you know him pretty well."

"We understand each other, all right," Drake said. "We should. We've been playing this game for a couple of years now."

That tidbit was going in her notes.

She shook her head in belated answer to his question about her means of transportation. "I don't have a horse," she explained. "I parked on a side road and hiked out here."

The day had been breathtakingly beautiful, before the clouds lowered and thickened and dumped rain. She'd hiked in all the western states and in Europe, and this was some gorgeous country. The Grand Tetons were just that. Grand.

"The nearest road is miles from here. You came all this way *on foot*?" Drake frowned at her. "Did my mother know you were crazy when she agreed to let you do your study here?"

"I actually enjoy hiking. A little rain doesn't bother me. I'll dry off back at the ranch."

"Back at the ranch?" he repeated slowly. Warily.

This was where she could tell him that his mother and hers were old friends, but she chose not to do it. She didn't want to take advantage of that relationship—or at least *appear* to be taking advantage of it. "That's a beautiful house you live in, by the way. Not what I expected to find on a place like this—chandeliers and oil paintings and wainscoting and all. Hardly the Ponderosa." She beamed a smile at Drake. "I was planning to camp out, but your mother generously invited me to stay on the ranch. My room has a wonderful view of the mountains. It's going to be glorious, waking up to that every morning."

Drake, she soon discovered, was still a few beats behind. "You're *staying* with us?"

"How else can I observe you in your native habitat?" Luce offered up another smile, her most innocent one. The truth was, she intended to camp some of the time, if only to avoid the long walk from the house. One of the main reasons she'd chosen this specific project was Drake himself, although she certainly wasn't going to tell him that! She'd known, even before Harry filled her in on the more personal aspects of his life, that he was an animal advocate, as well as a prominent rancher, that he had a degree in ecology. She'd first seen his name in print when she was still an undergrad, just a quote in an article, expressing his belief that running a large cattle operation could be done without endangering wildlife or the environment. Knowing that her mother and Blythe Carson were close had been a deciding factor, too, of course—a way of gaining access.

She allowed herself a few minutes to study the man. He sat on his horse confidently relaxed and comfortable in the saddle, the reins loosely held. The well-trained animal stood there calmly, clipping grass but not moving otherwise during their discussion.

Drake broke into her reverie by saying, "Guess I'd better take you back before something happens to you." He leaned toward her, reaching down. "Climb on."

She looked at the proffered hand and bit her lip, hesitant to explain that she'd ridden only once—an ancient horse at summer camp when she was twelve, and she'd been terrified the whole time.

No, she couldn't tell him that. Her pride wouldn't let her.

Besides, she wouldn't be steering the huge gelding; Drake would. And there was no denying the difficulties the weather presented.

She'd gotten some great footage during the afternoon and made a few notes, which meant the day wasn't a total loss.

"My backpack's heavy," she pointed out, her brief courage faltering. The top of that horse was pretty far off the ground. She could climb mountains, for Pete's sake, but that was different; she'd been standing on her own two feet the whole time.

At last, Drake smiled, and the impact of that smile was palpable. He was still leaning toward her, still holding out his hand. "Starburst's knees won't buckle under the weight of a backpack," he told her. "Or your weight, either."

The logic was irrefutable.

Drake slipped his booted foot out from the stirrup to make room for hers. "Come on. I'll haul you up behind me."

She handed up the backpack, sighed heavily. "Okay," she said. Then, gamely, she took Drake's hand. His grip was strong, and he swung her up behind him with no apparent effort.

It was easy to imagine this man working with horses and digging postholes for fences.

Settled on the animal's broad back, Luce had no choice

but to put her arms around his lean waist and hang on. For dear life.

The rain was coming down harder, and conversation was impossible.

Gradually, Luce relaxed enough to loosen her grip on Drake's middle.

A little, anyway.

Now that she was fairly sure she wasn't facing certain death, Luce allowed herself to enjoy the ride. Intrepid hiker though she was, the thought of trudging back to her car in a driving rain made her wince.

She hadn't missed the irony of the situation, either. She wanted to study wild horses, but she didn't know how to ride a tame one. Drake would be well within his rights to point that out to her, although she sensed, somehow, that he wouldn't.

When they finally reached the ranch house, he was considerate enough not to laugh when she slid clumsily off the horse and almost landed on her rear in a giant puddle. No, he simply tugged at the brim of his hat, suppressing a smile, and rode away without looking back.

Don't miss
ALWAYS A COWBOY
by New York Times *bestselling author*
Linda Lael Miller, available wherever HQN books
and ebooks are sold.